CW00670143

Sins of the Sarcophagus

A Small Town Murder Mystery

Kirsten Weiss

MISTERIO PRESS

Copyright

Copyright © 2023 by Kirsten Weiss

All rights reserved.

No part of this publication may be reproduced, distributed, or transmitted in any form or by any means, including photocopying, recording, or other electronic or mechanical methods, without the prior written permission of the publisher, except as permitted by U.S. copyright law. For permission requests, contact kweiss2001@kirstenweiss.com.

The story, all names, characters, and incidents portrayed in this production are fictitious. No identification with actual persons (living or deceased), places, buildings, and products is intended or should be inferred. AI has not been used in the conceptualization, generation, or drafting of this work.

Book Cover by Dar Albert

Illustrations licensed via DepositPhotos.com

misterio press / paperback edition August, 2023

ISBN-13: 978-1-962292-00-9

Visit the author website to sign up for updates on upcoming books and fun, free stuff: KirstenWeiss.com

Contents

About Sins of the Sarcophagus

DENIAL AIN'T JUST A river in Egypt...

Maddie Kosloski is about to unveil her new, expanded museum. But when the corpse of a local building inspector is discovered inside her prized Egyptian sarcophagus, Maddie's plans are thrown into disarray.

A modern mummy isn't all she's got on her hands. Running a non-profit paranormal museum is no get-rich-quick pyramid scheme. Maddie has stakeholders, more employees, and now donors to placate. Can she balance their demands and an off-the-books murder investigation?

Maddie must race against the clock to unearth a criminal more cunning than the Sphynx. But will the cost of unveiling this killer be more than she's willing to pay?

If you love laugh-out-loud mysteries with heart and a touch of the paranormal, you'll love *Sins of the Sarcophagus*, book 9 in the Perfectly Proper Paranormal Museum series of novels. (Written by a naturally flawed semi-intelligent human and not by AI).

Get cozy with this puzzling mystery today!

Special Offer!

THANK YOU FOR BUYING Sins of the Sarcophagus! I have a free gift if you'd like to read more light paranormal mystery! You can download *Fortune Favors the Grave*, a novella in my Tea and Tarot series, FREE right here —> Get the Book.

Will Abigail become a hostage to fortune?

Independent Abigail Beanblossom finally has the tearoom of her dreams, even if it is chock full of eccentric Tarot readers. But when her Tarot reading business partner, Hyperion Night, becomes embroiled in a rival's murder, Abigail discovers that true partnership is about more than profit and loss.

Escape into this hilarious mystery today!

chapter one

Egypt, circa 664 BC to 332 BC

This sarcophagus of an Egyptian high priest was removed from Egypt in 1872 by Percy Montrose. The amateur archaeologist ignored the warning that if even a grain of sand was removed from the tomb, he'd face the wrath of the gods and become a mummy himself. When he returned home to the United States, he was stricken by a fever and died.

The second spookiest place in San Benedetto is the Ladies Aid Lodge. And I'm pretty sure I'm *not* the only person who feels this way.

Butterflies churning in my stomach, I scanned the wide meeting hall, filled with chattering guests. Silken banners with cryptic symbols hung from the walls. Those belonged to Ladies Aid. Everything else was from my museum.

A terminal optimist, I'd planned on holding our soft opening inside the *actual* Paranormal History Museum. But getting a permit for pretty much anything in California was a long, random, and expensive process. A hiccup with the town's building inspectors had made a soft opening in the museum impossible.

And there was no point in dwelling on what I couldn't control. So I'd moved on to holding the soft opening for my new, expanded museum at the Ladies Aid Lodge.

Herb, my new curator, expounded to a group of reporters beside the Debunking Mediums Exhibit. The little man adjusted his coke bottle glasses and motioned expansively toward a vintage Houdini poster. A reporter ducked to avoid Herb's arm.

But the Egyptian magic exhibit that had the most gawkers. No surprise there—who didn't love a mummy? Not that I had an actual mummy—just the sarcophagus.

Naturally, it was cursed. If an object wasn't haunted, accursed, or unholy, it had no place in my museum.

I'd recently received a donation of such mind-boggling size I'd had to upgrade. Gone was the adorable little paranormal museum beside my friend's tearoom. Now we were a non-profit.

We'd snatched the local bowling alley out from under some developers to turn it into the new Paranormal History Museum. My mother had suggested the addition of "history." As much as I hated to admit it, the word did add a certain gravity to the place, even if we had kept the creepy dolls.

We'd also kept one of the bowling lanes—urban legend claimed it was haunted. I might not be able to stop change, but I was going to preserve what I could.

The transition to non-profit museum had forced me to step up my game in all sorts of unsettling ways. More staff, more professionalism. Many of the new objects in the museum were valuable and needed special care.

"Excuse me, Miss," a masculine voice rumbled. "Do you have a permit for this event?"

I flinched before recognizing the voice. "You're hilarious as a heart attack," I said dryly.

My tall, dark and handsome boyfriend, Detective Jason Slate, grinned down at me. "Too soon?"

I laughed and tugged the lapels of his charcoal suit jacket, drawing him closer. "Not in your case."

My gaze softened, my heart expanding at his presence. It was impossible not to. Jason was tall and solid and *here*.

He bent to kiss me, and I inhaled the scent of his spicy cologne. It was nice, calm, predictable, just like our relationship. Our lips touched, and a camera flashed. I pulled away, my face heating. "Ah..."

My newest employee, Chelsea, stalked toward us in a fitted little black dress. Her eyes narrowed, accentuating her thick, Cleopatra-style liner. The ode to Liz Taylor was *not* in honor of our new exhibit. She'd been wearing it at least since her job interview.

"Maddie, someone's spilled liquid at the base of the sarcophagus." The young woman flipped back her sleek, brown hair. "I *told* you we shouldn't have brought it here. It's too fragile."

My stomach tightened. The sarcophagus wasn't *that* fragile. But it *was* old. Regretfully, I stepped away from Jason. "I'd better take care of this."

"I'll manage the crowd," he said somberly. But his eyes, toffee flecked with gold, twinkled.

On tiptoe, I kissed his cheek. Then I hurried toward the Egyptian display, grabbing a stack of napkins off the food table along the way.

A folding wall painted like an Egyptian tomb formed a backdrop for the closed, upright sarcophagus. Dusty wooden crates, with straw and pottery spilling from them, lay scattered as if a tomb raider had just blown through. A black basalt Anubis statue as tall as Jason (six-foot-two) loomed over the display. The only modern element was a pedestal with a QR code for the audio tour.

The sarcophagus stood on a metal stand that tilted the wooden case back and off the floor. A muddy painting of a grim-looking ancient Egyptian with long, black braids glowered from the sarcophagus's lid.

I blotted the cool water puddling beneath the case. It was Chelsea who'd recommended keeping the sarcophagus off the floor. I'd been skeptical, but now I was glad the younger woman had been so insistent. Our new registrar—responsible for the care and upkeep of the collection—knew her business. Her youthful expertise was more than a little intimidating.

"The Rosicrucians will be so jealous," my mother purred. She studied the back of the sarcophagus and its painting of Maat, the Egyptian goddess of justice.

I straightened, crumpling the napkins in my hand. "The paranormal museum's not exactly in competition with them." Good thing, too. The collection of Egyptian artifacts at the Rosicrucian museum in nearby San Jose put ours to shame.

"Paranormal *History* Museum," she corrected, and I grimaced.

My mother's mouth quirked. She wore white slacks and a blue denim shirt. Her favorite squash-blossom necklace, the same color as the silvery threads in her cropped hair, encircled her throat. "I know for a fact the Rosicrucians offered to buy your Egyptian collection."

I rolled my eyes. Of *course* my mother knew about that. She was the co-president of Ladies Aid. That cabal knew everything that happened in our small central-California town.

She plucked a stuffed mushroom off her gold paper plate and nodded toward the long table in front of the dais. "The new caterer is amazing. I'm glad you're supporting local businesses."

The red-haired caterer, Alex, sliced ham off the bone. He scooped warmed peppers from a chafing dish and assembled a mini sandwich.

My stomach rumbled. I loved ham sandwiches. They reminded me of lunches with my father, who'd died years ago. But I'd been so busy, I hadn't had a chance to sample the food.

"Of course," my mother continued, "Melanie's catering will be considerably more upscale."

I bit back a sigh. My sister's wedding plans had gone light years over-the-top. Melanie overachieved at *overachieving*, and that included in her romantic life.

She was marrying a glamorous Italian count next month. And if my internal monologue was sounding a teeny bit like sour grapes... I'm ashamed to admit I *was* jealous. But at least I'd be getting a Sicilian vacation out of the affair.

A commotion near the Debunking Mediums exhibit caught my attention.

"What is Herb doing?" my mother asked.

His slight figure hopped sideways in a clumsy jig, his arms flailing spastically.

Good question. "Ah... Summoning a spirit?" He didn't seem to be in physical distress, but...

Herb stilled and dropped his arms. His head bowed as if the performance was complete.

I shifted. So he wasn't having some sort of attack. But he didn't look happy. He'd made a big transition recently too, shifting from paranormal collector to curator. I took a step toward him. "Mom, maybe I should...?" I trailed off.

Tall, muscular and blond, my former boyfriend and now former neighbor moved through the crowd. Mason's son, Jordan, trailed behind him. He was his father in miniature, right down to the black jeans and leather motorcycle jacket, though Mason's hair was pulled back in a ponytail. The pre-teen's shoulders hunched, his hands in the pockets of his jeans.

I stopped in my tracks, my heart pinching. We hadn't spoken much since things had gone so badly with Belle, his fiancée and the mother of his child. She'd broken off the engagement and abandoned both Mason and their son. But if he was here—

Arctic eyes serious, Mason caught my gaze. He smiled, then bent and said something to his son. Jordan darted toward the food table. Mason strode toward us, and my breath caught.

Mason's motorcycle shop stood next door to my old museum. He and Jordan and Jordan's mother had lived above it. And I'd sort of been responsible for Jordan's mother no longer being in the picture.

My friend Harper Caldarelli stepped between us. "There you are." She brushed a length of dark hair off her shoulder. "The museum's killing it tonight. All of Town Hall is here."

Harper was dressed professionally in a sleek forest-green business suit that set off all her curves. But as a town councilwoman and financial advisor, she always dressed to impress.

"Thanks to you." I glanced past her. Mason had stopped to talk to an elderly woman in a blue knit suit.

"And that includes the inspection department," Harper added pointedly.

I growled and refocused on Harper. If it wasn't for the inspectors, we'd be in the actual museum.

My mother nudged my arm. "It wouldn't hurt to make nice."

My scowl deepened. *Make nice?*

In my old career, I'd worked in developing countries. Getting things approved by government agencies was a matter of who you knew or who you paid. The corruption was a large part of the reason these countries were euphemistically called "developing" rather than "developed."

Harper blew out a noisy breath, her olive skin darkening. "It's not entirely the inspection team's fault things got delayed. The head inspector quit without a word to anyone."

"I heard he ran off with his new girlfriend," my mother said.

"The point is," Harper continued doggedly, "we're short staffed."

"*We?*" I still found it mildly hilarious that my friend was now a town bigwig. In high school, Harper had slipped a carp into a classroom's A/C vent over spring break. The result had shut down the room for days.

The corners of her mouth tipped upward. "Okay, *they*. But sort of *we*. And I got them to agree to send someone out tomorrow."

"Tomorrow's Sunday," I said, shocked. The inspectors *never* worked Sundays.

Harper's grin broadened. "Like your mom said, it doesn't hurt to make nice."

"I'll say hi," I grumbled.

"You owe me." A woman's voice rose angrily above the crowd.

The caterer hurried around the long table and touched a slender woman's elbow. She was about his age, in her mid-fifties, with curling brown hair. Beside the big man, she seemed small and fragile.

Head bent, the caterer said something to her. She stiffened and strode into the crowd. Mouth compressing, the caterer returned to his station.

My mother tsked. "Marital troubles."

"You know her?" I asked.

"Wynnona Cookson," my mother said, "your caterer's wife."

I hadn't even known he *had* a wife. Trying not to look impressed at my mom's intel-gathering powers, I moved toward the Debunking exhibit.

A man in his forties, his hair prematurely white, stepped in front of me. "Nice crowd," Frank Frost said.

I extended my hand, and we shook. "Thanks again for sponsoring the event," I said.

Frank threw back his head and laughed, a great, rolling chuckle. "Are you kidding? A cryogenics-slash-cryotherapy company sponsoring a paranormal museum is a natural fit. Most people think what Frostova does is creepy."

I thought it was creepy. Cryonics froze the body after death. Cryotherapy was a cold therapy that was supposed to offer health benefits. Neither appealed. But I appreciated the sponsorship.

"Any word on those permits?" he asked.

I grimaced. "I was just going to go make nice with the inspection team." I nodded toward a cluster of bureaucrats beside the catering table.

"You wouldn't believe the grief they gave me when I was setting up." He shook his head. "But Frostova got through it. Your museum will too."

"That's—"

A woman's scream split the air. People muttered, the crowd shifting.

"Oh my God," a woman cried. "He's real."

At the Egyptian exhibit, young Jordan held the sarcophagus lid awkwardly against him. The top of the lid angled above his head, its base resting against the floor. A mummy stood stiffly inside the open case.

I frowned. I hadn't put a mummy in there. Who'd added the mummy?

"Put that back," Chelsea snapped, striding toward the boy. "You'll damage the lid."

The mummy's knees buckled. Loops of damp, white fabric sagged downward, exposing a man's gray face and staring eyes. The mummy tumbled onto the linoleum floor and rolled onto his back. More fabric pulled loose across his chest, exposing an SF *Giants* logo tee.

I stopped breathing. I think my heart stopped beating too.

That was no mummy.

"I just wanted to see inside," Jordan said weakly. He shifted the lid against his body.

Jason appeared at my side. Gently, he edged me sideways and knelt by the mummy. He pulled out his phone. "Maddie, get everyone back."

"But that's not—" I pointed shakily.

"Get everyone back," he repeated. "This is a crime scene."

chapter two

TALKING BOARDS

USA, *circa* 1855 - 1896

Most people are familiar with the Ouija board, introduced by the Kennard Novelty Company in 1890. However, it faced stiff competition from other talking board manufacturers. These colorful pieces of pop culture are not just glimpses into the history of the spiritualist movement, they're also works of art.

I adjusted a stanchion and clipped the velvet rope into its brass hook. Not that the barrier was really needed. The guests had moved back on Jason's command.

My young museum assistant, Leo, gently took the sarcophagus lid from Jordan. He laid it on the floor.

Chelsea made an exclamation of outrage and knelt beside it, her black dress bunching about her slender thighs. She shot an evil look at Leo, then she scanned the painted lid for damage.

Leo shrugged and swiped shock of near-black hair out of his eyes. My assistant was as new to professional museum-ing as I was. He probably should have used gloves to move the lid. But Jordan had already been holding it in his bare hands.

I rubbed the back of my neck. "Why does that mummy look familiar?" I muttered, studying the dripping man on the wooden floor.

"And why is he so *damp*?" My mother toyed with her silver necklace.

Jason squatted beside the body. His charcoal suit jacket strained against his muscular back. "Do you know him?" he asked without looking up.

I gasped. I *did* know him. "That's my first inspector," I blurted. "Building inspector, I mean. The one who, er, quit."

I'd been torn between relief and annoyance when it had happened. He'd been a hard ass. Now I felt bad I couldn't even remember his name.

A woman cried out, and I glanced her way. Her freckled face pale, Wynnona pressed a hand to her mouth. She reeled backward.

Jason stood. "I'd like to ask that no one speak to each other until they can make their statement to a police officer," he said loudly.

Guests murmured in response, and he sighed. I shook my head. There was no way he could stop everyone from talking.

"It's important no one's memories or impressions get tainted," I said over the muttering. "The more we talk to each other about it, the more our own memories will be contaminated."

Jason's expression flickered, and I shrugged guiltily. I might have stepped on his toes by explaining the no-talking rule, but people would be more willing to cooperate if they understood why. Though it didn't seem like I'd made much of an impression.

"What about the curse?" a woman shouted.

Outside, a siren sounded faintly and grew in volume. Two uniformed police officers arrived and Jason motioned them toward us.

A tall blonde in a blue sequined dress strode into the hall behind the officers. She scanned the crowd. Her gaze fell on me, and her ice-blue eyes narrowed.

I swallowed, sweat breaking out on my forehead. Detective Laurel Hammer had never liked me. Not even when we were kids. She'd taken such offense to my existence, she'd once jammed me into a gym locker. It had taken a team of firemen to extract me.

Trying to look inconspicuous, I edged from the velvet rope around the Egyptian scene. Laurel stalked toward me.

A tiny white-haired lady in a pale blue suit materialized by my elbow. All the women from Ladies Aid had gotten free passes to the opening. "Well," she huffed. "Depositing the body here was a mistake. Between Maddie and Ladies Aid, the killer doesn't stand a chance."

The skin around Laurel's nostrils whitened, and my neck turtled inward. The detective had heard.

"How lucky we are to have a detective on the scene," my mother said, her voice carrying.

Laurel's face reddened.

"Two detectives now," my mother hastily amended. She patted the white-haired lady's arm. "Let's let the authorities do their job. And Maddie, of course," she added in a lower voice.

But it wasn't low enough for Jason not to hear. His eyebrows skyrocketed.

My face heated. *Thanks, Mom.*

On the bright side—and there's almost always a bright side—the soft opening got more press than I'd expected. We'd made the national news, even earning a shout-out from a late night cable talk show.

Need I add the show was a comedy?

But a man had been killed, and someone had put his body in the museum's sarcophagus. There was nothing funny about the situation. It was very, very bad.

"The police can't just *take* that sarcophagus," Chelsea said, her voice shrill over the phone.

Wincing, I nudged my cell phone farther from the bowl on my laminate kitchen table. Watery morning sunlight streamed through the blue curtains, illuminating the piles of dishes in the sink.

"It's over two-thousand years old," she continued. I'd swear my phone vibrated with indignation.

"Unfortunately, the police can and did." I jammed my spoon into the bowl of granola and yogurt.

"That sarcophagus needs special care," she bleated. "God knows how much damage the water did to it. I need to examine it."

A point which she'd made—at length—to the police when they'd taken away the sarcophagus. "I'll contact the police station this morning and ask about its status."

"They wouldn't do this to the De Young," she fumed.

I doubted that. Or maybe they *wouldn't* have confiscated an ancient relic from a more prestigious museum. I'd long since given up the fantasy that government bureaucracies worked on a basis of fairness and merit. *Who you knew* and all that.

Acid burned my gut, and I rubbed my stomach. I'd known accepting the donation that had expanded the collection would bring new challenges. I hadn't known freaking out over ancient relics would be one of them.

True, there were tens of thousands of sarcophagi in the world. Also true, the Paranormal Museum's wasn't a particularly outstanding example. But it had survived over two thousand years. I'd hate to be the one responsible for its demise.

"I told you," Chelsea said, "it needed to be—"

"I'm going to call the police now." I rose and balanced my granola on top of a ziggurat of bowls. "Talk to you later." I disconnected, muttered a few choice swear words, and called Jason.

"You can't have the sarcophagus back yet," he said without preamble. "We're sending it to a forensics team in Sacramento."

"They won't have anything to examine if it falls apart due to water damage."

He sucked in a breath. "Is that possible?"

I dropped heavily into the kitchen chair. "According to my registrar, yes. Is there any way Chelsea can get in there to assess the damage and give your team instructions on care?"

Jason exhaled slowly. "I'll see what I can do." He hung up.

I drummed my fingers on the small table. True, a present-day murder took precedence over an ancient blinged-out casket.

But it was *my* blinged-out casket. Well, the museum's. And it was irritating that people thought they could go around dumping bodies in it.

I rose and checked the clock on my phone: 11:11. I'd gotten up late since I'd stayed up past midnight dealing first with the police, then with Ladies Aid. But I was still on time to make my follow-up meeting with the caterer.

I drove to his workspace inside a corrugated steel building in a business park. It was the same park where Herb kept his own special collection—or one of them. I wondered if Herb's plans for it had changed since he'd become a full-time curator. Or was he still selling his artifacts on the side?

I caught myself sinking low in the seat of my pickup as I cruised past Herb's warehouse. Sure, Herb was working for me full-time now. But he got defensive about his collection.

At least he'd stopped pestering me about buying Dion Fortune's scrying mirror. It would have made an excellent addition to our Twentieth Century Occultists exhibit. But with the expansion and new employees, we didn't have a *centime* to spare.

The spaces in front of the catering office were empty, and I parked. A stenciled pink cupcake grinned from the glass door. I strolled inside, setting off an electronic chime.

"Hello?" I called, setting my phone on a pink table.

Alex hurried from an inner room. He was in his mid-fifties and nearly six-foot tall, with fading, red hair. "Oh, hey. You're right on time." The bearlike man wiped his hands on his black apron, spattered with flour. His biceps bulged beneath his white t-shirt.

"Mind if we talk in the kitchen?" He angled his head toward the doorway he'd just emerged from. "I got thrown off schedule after last night. The police kept me late, and I'm behind."

"Sure, no problem."

I followed him into a room gleaming with metal tables and racks and ovens and a giant walk-in freezer. The kitchen smelled of baking sugar, and my stomach growled. I should have eaten that granola.

Alex handed me a hairnet. "Uh, do you mind?"

There were some people I'd feel insecure around wearing a hairnet. The caterer was not one of them. "Not at all." I slipped it on, tucking my ponytail beneath the white cap.

"And your shoes?" He extended blue paper booties.

I forced a smile. Since I hadn't planned on sticking my shoes into any of the food, this seemed excessive. But it was his show. Leaning against a gray-painted wall, I pulled on the booties.

I straightened off the wall and pulled a folded check from my Paranormal Museum hoodie. "First, here's the final payment." Arm extended, I stepped closer, onto a black fatigue mat.

"Thanks." Taking the check, Alex glanced at it and slipped it into his apron pocket.

"Police action aside, the opening went well. Your food was a hit."

His laugh was caustic. "I don't think anyone is talking about the catering today."

"No…" I trailed off, my stomach sinking. That building inspector… But what had happened wasn't my fault.

I just wish I knew how he'd ended up in my sarcophagus. I shook myself. "I guess not. But we'll both get another chance at the Grand Opening."

"Have you finalized the date?"

No. We still hadn't gotten final approval from the building inspectors. "An inspector's at the museum today. But I'm still aiming for October 31st."

"That's in six weeks," he said, expression doubtful.

"It'll be fine." *Just fine…* I *hoped* it would be fine.

But how could I pass up a grand opening on Halloween? Once Halloween was over, we'd be in the thick of holiday parties. Holiday madness would put an end to any interest in our grand opening. I had to get it done by October 31st or wait until next year.

Alex shrugged his muscular shoulders. "Okay then." He walked to a metal table. "You know our cancellation policy."

My mouth went dry. I knew I'd eat the down payment if we canceled. So we were *not* going to cancel. "Are you working alone here today?" I glanced around the gleaming kitchen.

There wasn't a speck of flour on a single metal counter or any other post-baking detritus. I couldn't pour *milk* without spilling.

"I'm here alone most days," he said.

"What about your staff?"

"Don't have any. I use temps for the events, like yours. But the business is growing, thanks to people like you. Soon, I'll have to start hiring permanent staff to help out here."

"The temps worked fine last night," I said. "But there'll be a larger group at the Grand Opening in October."

"Don't worry," he said. "I'll manage."

"Hey," I said casually. "I have to ask. Did you notice anything odd when you were setting up last night?"

"Odd?" He lowered a stand mixer into a bowl.

"People who didn't belong."

Alex shook his head. "You were there."

"Not the whole time." I'd been in and out—mostly *out* dealing with Ladies Aid. I'd given that crew a private tour of the collection when we'd set it up the day before. I'd caught several members sneaking back in, hoping for a glimpse of a grisly apparition. I'd done my best to keep them out of the caterer's hair.

He clucked his tongue. Grabbing a bleach wipe from a nearby container, he wiped up a speck of batter from the metal table. "I told the police everything I know." He dropped the wipe into a nearby garbage can.

"What *do* you know?"

"Nothing." Alex snapped the top of the bleach wipe container shut.

"Oh." It had been a longshot anyway. Moving a body into that sarcophagus would have required privacy, and there hadn't been much of it in that hall. So when had it gotten in there?

"Why?" he asked. "You're not really investigating? I thought those women with Ladies Aid were joking."

I took an involuntary step backward and pressed my palm to my chest. "Me? No, of course not. But you know Ladies Aid." I shifted my weight. "Or maybe you don't. They're the hidden power in this town."

"That, I *had* heard." He turned on the stand mixer filled with rectangles of butter.

"Yeah," I said over the whir of the mixer. "Well, the point is, they took a corpse in their Grand Hall personally. And my mom's the co-president. She's upset, and I guess I want to help put her mind at ease."

"Sounds more like a job for the police."

My face warmed. "Oh, it is." Jason had been there when the body was found. He was a good cop, and though I hated to admit it, Laurel was too.

He switched off the mixer. "You sure? Because I heard some of the women from Ladies Aid talking about you being a private detective on the side."

"What? No. The police are on it. I'm just..." I studied my tennis shoes in their plastic booties. "I didn't know the inspector well. He wasn't a friend. Part of me says it's none of my business. But someone dressed him up like a mummy and shoved him in my—in the museum's sarcophagus."

And it wasn't *right*. Maybe that was ego on my part—maybe putting him in *my* museum was what seemed so wrong. But I thought it was more than that, and I didn't know how to explain, or at least how to explain without sounding like a diva. "It makes you think," I finished lamely.

"About what?"

About...? This is what happened when I let my mouth run ahead of my brain. "About, ah, how it got into that sarcophagus. I mean, it wasn't in there when I brought the sarcophagus over from our warehouse on Friday. We would have noticed. So someone had to have put it in sometime between when we finished with the set-up Friday night. You were there—"

"We left Ladies Aid on Friday together," he said, his voice hardening.

"Yeah, I know. I'm just saying, that's roughly twenty-four hours be-tween when we left and when the body was discovered. And I don't see any of the women from Ladies Aid pulling off a body disposal."

And no, I wasn't prejudiced against little old ladies as killers. I just couldn't believe Ladies Aid would do anything so gauche. "Hauling a dead body around takes strength. Or a dolly."

"Look, I didn't see anything. I'm sorry."

I grimaced. "No, there's nothing to be sorry for. You're right. You wouldn't have seen anything." No one would try to stuff a body into that sarcophagus under the caterer's nose. "It's not like Ladies Aid is Fort Knox. Someone must have come in before you began setting up on Saturday."

I'd be having a long talk with my mother about just who had access. Even though Jason had already taken statements, he didn't have the "in" with Ladies Aid that I did.

The electronic chime rang in the other room. Alex glanced toward the kitchen door.

I drew a long breath. *In for a penny, in for a pound.* Since I was here, I might as well learn what I could. "When exactly *did* you arrive Saturday?"

Wynnona, in a t-shirt and skinny jeans, walked into the kitchen. Her eyes were red, and her heart-shaped face pink and splotchy. "Alex—" She stopped short, swaying at the edge of a black fatigue mat. "Oh. I didn't realize." She scraped her curling brown hair out of her eyes. "I just wanted to get something from the freezer." She moved past us.

He stiffened. "Wait, you can't—"

She turned to him. "Can't?"

His shoulders relaxed. "Of course. Sorry. Take whatever you want."

And then Wynnona seemed to take notice of me. She cocked her head.

"Hi." I waved, my hand chest height. "I'm Maddie. From the Paranormal History Museum. We met—"

Her face spasmed. "Never mind." Head down, she hurried back the way she came. The front door chime rang.

"My wife," he said shortly. "She worries. She's been upset since last night. We left San Francisco last year to get away from the crime."

"Of course," I murmured. "Er, so what time did you arrive at Ladies Aid last night?"

"Five o'clock sharp."

"Right. Right. Thanks." We finalized the details for our Halloween grand opening, and I left the shop. The door chime pinged behind me. I paused to shield my eyes against the sun.

Breathing heavily, Wynnona stood, one hand braced on the top of a red minivan. I gnawed the inside of my lip. Her "upset" seemed like more than just a reaction to a local crime, startling as it had been.

And it was none of my business. Jason and Laurel were on the case. But I couldn't ignore someone in obvious distress. Slowly, I walked toward the caterer's wife. "Are you all right?"

Wynnona coughed. "Yes." She straightened off the van, her smile tight. "You must think I'm crazy. It was your coffin Ira was found in. If anyone should be upset, it's you."

Sarcophagus. I mentally kicked myself. Who cared what it was called? "Ira?"

"That was his name. Ira Myatt. You didn't know?"

"I'd forgotten," I said guiltily. "Did you know him well?"

"No. Not really." She shook her head. "It was tough moving to a new town at our age, making friends. I—I'd thought Ira had become a friend, and then when he disappeared..." Her breath hitched.

I leaned closer, my stomach tightening. It had been obvious she'd known Ira. But I couldn't resist asking for more. "How did you meet him?"

"When he came to inspect the business." Wynnona nodded toward the metal building. "He was very... direct. I liked him. Alex did too. I hope they catch whoever did this to him." She opened the door and climbed inside the minivan.

I walked to my pickup and climbed inside. But I hesitated, keys in the ignition, until she drove away.

For me, the inspector had been an irritant, an impediment. But he'd been a person, with hopes and fears and friends. And someone had killed him and put him in my sarcophagus dressed as a mummy, a joke.

But it wasn't a joke. At least one person was mourning him. And it wasn't funny at all.

chapter three

THUNDERSTONES

Ghana, circa 2 million BC

Legend has it that thunder stones are formed by lightning striking the earth. The stones are believed to possess spiritual properties. They are used for a variety of magical purposes by traditional healers and spiritualists in Nigeria and Ghana.

My stomach grumbled. In need of comfort food, I drove to Adele Nakamoto's tearoom, the Fox and Fennel.

And since I no longer worked next door, I hogged a spot on the street instead of parking in back. No more servant's entrance for me. *Ha.* It was ridiculously satisfying.

Stepping from my pickup, I paused on the sidewalk and stretched. Burgundy plum tree leaves lay scattered across the bricks outside Mason's motorcycle shop.

I stared blindly at the custom bikes gleaming in his windows. Mason's son had probably come to my museum expecting some cheap supernatural thrills. He'd gotten a lot more than he'd bargained for when he'd opened that sarcophagus.

The faint sounds of hammering rang out from next door, and suddenly I was back inside the original museum, folds of plastic sheeting dangling between it and the tearoom next door.

Nostalgia misted my eyes, and I turned from the windows. The new museum was bigger and better, but I still felt a twinge at the loss of my funky, low-budget original.

But life moved on. Adele was expanding her tearoom into the old museum, and that was a good thing. It was irrational to get emotional about change. I strode past the paper-covered windows of my old museum and into the tearoom.

Adele bustled to the hostess stand, and I smiled. I don't have a lot of people I'd call friends. Adele and Harper were two. We'd been friends since grade school and had each other's backs. Her coffee-colored eyes were wide with concern.

"What have you heard?" she asked, her black brows drawing downward. "The police questioned Dieter and me last night, but we didn't see a thing." She smoothed the front of her Jackie Kennedy-style powder-blue suit.

My cheeks warmed. I'd been so distracted last night, I hadn't even noticed Adele and her husband in the crowd. I shook my head. "I haven't heard anything."

"It's not going to give you any problems at the board meeting," she said, "will it?"

I frowned. My upcoming board meeting—the museum's first—was the last of my worries. "I don't see why it would. It wasn't the museum's fault someone put a body in our sarcophagus."

The bookcase door swung inward, the volume of the hammering rising. Dieter slipped through the opening. White dust coated his spiky brown hair. "Hey, Mad Dog. Quite a scene last night. Leave it to you to maximize the show."

My mouth pinched. It wasn't funny.

"Dieter," my friend scolded. "You know Maddie didn't—"

He looped a bronzed arm over her shoulder, depositing plaster dust on her suit. "Just kidding." He pressed a kiss to her forehead. "What's up?"

"I was hoping to get a sandwich," I said.

Adele scanned the busy tearoom, and her forehead creased. "We're full up. But I can bring you something to go."

"Roast beef?" I asked.

She nodded. Pivoting on her low heels, she bustled down the hallway into the kitchen.

I hesitated. *Oh, the hell with it.* I wasn't going to feel right until I knew what had happened to Ira. "How well did you know that inspector?" I asked Dieter. Adele's husband was a contractor, which was convenient for Adele. He'd also warned me about Ira before our inspection had begun.

"Only on the job," he said. "Ira was a real hard ass." He rubbed his chin. "It is strange though..."

"What?"

"Well, when you were trying to open the first museum, you found a body in it. And now that you're opening the second, you found another body. Well, a mummy."

"Ira's body wasn't *in* the museum," I said, shrill. At the tables, several women glanced our way. In a lower voice, I continued, "It was in the Ladies Aid lodge."

He angled his head. "Yeah, but—"

My phone rang in the back pocket of my jeans, and I yanked it out. *Leo.* I gusted a breath. "Hello?"

"Hey," my assistant said, "the inspector's finally here."

"Good." Then we could finally finish this. I glared at Dieter. And my museum was *not* in the habit of attracting murder victims.

Leo cleared his throat. "Uh, maybe not so good. There's a problem."

I'm not a big one for shouting at people, unless it's to warn them to leap out of the way of something large and fast-moving. But I was having a hard time restraining myself.

My fists clenched in my hoodie's pockets. "Because the building was built in the fifties," I said, "we're grandfathered in. We're only required to put twenty percent of our remodel costs toward additional ADA compliance. We don't *have* to install a ramp inside the building. We've got an elevator."

I motioned to the wheelchair elevator. The entry to the museum was at ground level. Guests could descend via stairs or the elevator to the exhibits half-a-floor lower, where the bowling lanes had been.

If we installed a ramp to get to the museum proper, we'd have to wrap it around the entire bowling alley. Otherwise, the ramp would be so steep wheelchairs would rocket into oblivion. Wrapping the ramp would mean tearing out all our existing construction along those walls. It was impossible.

From our position at the museum's lobby, the inspector, Leo, and I looked out over the labyrinth of dark walls. Dieter and his team had built them over all the bowling lanes but one.

The new corridors were charcoal colored with white crown molding for an atmosphere of charming gloom. Narratives stenciled in white decorated the walls above the exhibits. The bowling alley's industrial lighting had been replaced with mismatched, salvaged chandeliers.

The deeper one walked into the maze of exhibits, the darker and more cramped the corners became. The effect created an eerie claustrophobia, until one emerged into the natural lighting of the museum shop. Guests would leave on an up note that would hopefully entice them to buy. Or at least later.

The inspector, Ronald Batson, stuck out his angular jaw. "That's not on the form." He was a few years older than me, in his late thirties, and a couple inches taller—I guessed about five-nine. His auburn hair reared up around the sunglasses shoved high on his head.

This could *not* be happening. I tugged on my hoodie strings. "What do you mean it's not on the form?" I asked, exasperated. "It's in the regulations."

"It needs to be on the form," he said stubbornly, brandishing a clipboard.

"How can I put a regulation on the form? It's *your* form!"

Beside me, Leo cleared his throat. My youthful assistant shook the mass of near-black hair out of his eyes.

And my last words *might* have verged on shouting. I breathed more slowly. "Look." I pulled my phone from my hoodie's pocket and found the regulation on line. "Right there. It's on your website. ADA compliance and grandfathered buildings." I handed him the phone.

He glanced at my phone and handed it back. "I'm not responsible for the website."

Deep breaths. I jammed my fists into my hoodie's pockets. There was a solution to everything. I just had to calm down and find it.

"Our architect assured me that this was all compliant," I said in a level tone. "His plans were approved by your department. The stamp's right there. Ira looked everything over, and he didn't see anything wrong with the elevator." I pointed at the architectural drawing on his clipboard.

"Yeah." His sunburnt brow furrowed. "But Ira's dead."

Why had he sounded like that was *my* fault? I forced a smile. "I'm sorry for your loss. And I should have said that up front."

"Thanks."

"When Ira disappeared like that," I said craftily, "it must have caused a lot of problems in your department."

"You have no idea," he said in a dull tone.

So much for sleuthing. I tried again on the permitting front. "There must be a solution. *Someone* in your department approved these plans. It isn't right to ask me to change them now."

Ronald's head lowered. "Yeah. Well." He scratched his head. "I think we need to talk to someone in permitting."

"Great. Who?"

"Janice."

"Okay. Should I call for an appointment? How do I explain this to her?" Because it was all too easy for me to imagine getting the runaround. I'd been getting that a lot lately.

Ronald sighed. "I'll do it. I'll call you later." He stuck his pen in his clipboard and left.

Leo clapped my shoulder. "It'll work out. They approved the plans. The guy's wrong."

I pressed my lips together. The alternative was that the *approval* had been wrong. And in the world of government bureaucracies, I'd be on the losing end of that battle.

"Also, Herb wants to talk to you." Leo stuffed his hands into the pockets of his black jeans. "And there's a reporter here."

"What?" *What reporter?*

A door snicked open. Chelsea hurried toward us from behind the old bowling alley counter. Today's little black dress was slightly less elegant but equally fashionable as last night's. A white headband with sixties' vibes held back her smooth, near black hair. And how *did* she get her Cleopatra eyeliner so perfect? It wasn't fair.

"Well?" she demanded. "What did the police say about the sarcophagus?"

I did *not* need this right now. But she was doing her job, caring for the collection. *I am calm and relaxed.* I exhaled slowly. "Nothing, yet."

"But you said—"

Raising my hands in a warding fashion, I forced a smile. "I talked to the lead detective. He said he'd discuss it with the Sacramento forensics team."

Chelsea's brown eyes widened. "They're not moving it all the way to Sacramento, are they? That sarcophagus needs special handling."

"I know. Jason knows. I've made it clear that their investigation is at risk if the sarcophagus falls apart. He'll call me once a decision's been made."

She clutched her head, rumpling the white band. "This is a disaster. That's one of our most valuable pieces."

"At least it's not the oldest," Leo said.

She whirled on him. "Those thunderstones are a dime a dozen. People used them to grind grain. The reason they've survived from the paleolithic era is because they're nearly impossible to break."

And it was our good luck that they were used today in spellcasting rituals. The stones helped round out our Africa exhibit.

"I need to be there when they're transporting the sarcophagus," Chelsea said, "to ensure it's stored properly. And I need to be there when they're examining it."

"I can't promise anything," I said. "It's not up to me."

"I can't *believe* this." She stormed around the counter and into a back room. A door slammed.

"She's a little tense," Leo said.

"But she does know how to manage the artifacts," I said hollowly.

Transitioning from a small-town attraction to a "real" museum had been a heavy lift. There'd been a lot to learn. I'd soon discovered I didn't have the bandwidth to do it all.

So I'd decided to stick with my strengths—the business and marketing. But it wasn't easy for me to relinquish control, or to admit that the way I'd cared for artifacts in the past hadn't always been optimal. Or that someone so much younger knew more than me.

Herb strode into the lobby. "Ah, Maddie. Did you see my request to attend that curation certification course in San Francisco? I left it on your desk."

Augh! I calculated the odds of successfully fleeing to my office and shutting everyone out. Needless to say, they were low.

Why was everything happening at once? *I am calm. I am relaxed. I am in charge.*

"Yes, I'm sorry." I rubbed my forehead. It was damp. "I was a little surprised. You know more about these exhibits than anyone. Are you sure you need a certificate in curation?"

"Knowing the artifacts isn't the same as knowing how to present them."

"Okay. Look. I'll need to check the budget." Though I had a pretty good idea the funds wouldn't be there. I couldn't even afford that scrying mirror he'd been trying to pawn off on me for years.

"The certification is very important," Herb said shrilly. "Not only will it expand my knowledge, but I can make all sorts of contacts."

"Yes, but—"

"I need this certification." My curator's narrow chin quivered. "No one will take me seriously without at *least* a certificate in curation."

"I take you seriously," I said.

"Oh, please," he huffed and folded his arms over his tweed jacket. "You know less than I do. And I'll need to enroll soon to make the upcoming semester."

I *did* know less than Herb when it came to curation. "Okay, I'll check the budget." And yes, this was a cop-out. And yes, I was putting him off. In fairness though, I had a lot going on.

Herb snorted. Pivoting, he strode from the lobby.

Massaging the bridge of my nose, I turned to Leo. "Reporter?"

"In the gift shop."

"Gotcha." I strode into the gift shop. *Calm and relaxed.*

Mike was a freckled man with a boyish face and an earnest expression. It no doubt tricked the innocent and unwary into revealing all sorts of dirty secrets.

I wove through the round tables, laden with Paranormal History Museum clothing and books and Tarot cards. "Hi, Mike." I extended my hand warily. It would be nice to believe he was here to give the museum free publicity. But alas, I fell into neither the innocent nor the unwary categories.

He set his phone on the glass counter, and we shook hands. "Hi, Maddie. Quite an opening last night." The reporter's thick, wool jacket was slung over the old-fashioned register. He wore a plain white, button up shirt over his khakis.

I scrubbed a hand over my face. "Soft opening," I corrected. Our actual grand opening would *have* to be an improvement over last night's debacle.

"So," he said, grinning. "A cursed mummy."

I folded my arms. "He wasn't technically a mummy." At least I didn't think he was. "And the sarcophagus was cursed, not the person inside it. But yes, it was awful. You were there," I reminded him.

"Cursed to turn anyone who violated the tomb into a mummy themselves."

Uneasy, I shifted my weight. "That's the gist of the curse. Broadly."

"Hm." He pulled a phone from the back pocket of his khakis and touched its screen. "Hey, you don't mind if I record this, do you? Great," he said before I could respond. "I understand the victim was the museum's original inspector?"

My stomach tightened. "Yes."

"Any idea how he ended up in your coffin?"

"Sarcophagus. It's a sar—" I shook my head. "Never mind. And no, of course not. This has been a horrible shock, and our hearts go out to his family."

Did Ira even have a family? Not knowing that made my stomach twist. I felt like it was something I *should* know.

And why did I feel like Ira and I had a relationship by virtue of his body being in my sarcophagus? Because I certainly hadn't felt a connection when he'd been inspecting my museum. I'd just wanted him done and gone.

"Pretty weird he was dressed up like a mummy," the reporter said.

"Yeah," I said, drawing out the word. "It was so on the nose as to be—"

He cocked his head. "What?"

Inspired. But I didn't want to say that aloud. It would sound flippant, and I hadn't meant it that way.

"Who do you think put the mummy there?" he asked.

That was an excellent question. And it was one I was going to find the answer to. My jaw set. Because figuring things out was one of my strengths as well.

chapter four

DIVINATION BOWL

Nigeria, circa 1920

Divination bowls were used to store the ritual tools of a Yoruba high priest. This bowl depicts scenes from everyday life. The lid represents various totem animals. The face on the side represents Orunmila, the spirit of wisdom, divinity and prophecy in the Yoruba religion.

Leaving Leo and Chelsea to their work, I drove to the Ladies Aid lodge. It was a deceptively innocent looking blocky, two-story building out of the fifties. I stepped up to the black front door. Ignoring the brass door knocker, I rang the bell.

After a few moments, the door creaked open. My mother, trim in khaki slacks and a denim shirt, peered out and blinked in the sunshine. "Thank goodness you're here." She grabbed my elbow and tugged me inside.

"Huh?" I shuffled back a step, but she pulled me inexorably forward. "What's going on?" I asked.

"Since your exhibits are still in our hall—"

"Sorry about that." I tugged at my hoodie's collar. "The police asked me to leave everything."

"I know." She lead me down the hall lined with photos of past Ladies Aid presidents. "But now we have to cram into the library for our meetings."

And now Ladies Aid was suffering for doing the museum a favor. What was it they said about good deeds and punishment? "I know it's inconvenient, and—"

She opened an arched wooden door. Books and paintings lined the walls, covered in rose-patterned wallpaper. The usual groupings of high-backed chairs had been shoved to the sides. Women sat in rows of folding chairs facing a podium.

"Oh." My mouth puckered. I stopped short. "You meant now." They were all in the library *now*.

Cora, my mother's zaftig co-president, stood behind the podium. In her blue velvet caftan and matching turban, she looked like a circus psychic. She brandished a gavel in my direction. "Right on time. Maddie, what have you learned?"

Hips swiveled in chairs. Eyes turned to study me.

I gulped. "Ah..."

"About the body," my mother whispered.

The guy had been found less than eighteen hours ago. Why did they expect me to know anything? "His name was Ira Myatt."

A hatchet-faced woman named Eliza snorted. Her blue suit looked so stiff it might have been holding the bulky woman up. "We *know* that. He was San Benedetto's Chief Building Inspector."

"The thing is, the police are only at the beginning of their investigation," I hedged.

"That much is obvious," Eliza said. "But where are *you*?"

I shuffled my feet on the thin carpet. "Me?"

Okay, yes. I *was* asking some discreet questions about Ira's death. We were bonded by that sarcophagus. But I hadn't informed Ladies Aid of my activities, such as they were.

I guess my mom knew me well enough to guess I might stick my nose in. But I couldn't believe she'd put me on the spot.

"Because of you," Eliza said, "someone used our lodge as a dumping ground. For a *body*."

"That's hardly Madelyn's fault," my mother said stiffly.

I winced. My mother and Cora had wrested control of Ladies Aid from Eliza not too long ago. Feelings were still running high. So maybe she *would* throw me to the wolves. I tried not to take that personally.

A wispy, white-haired woman sighed. "I suppose the killer saw that fancy coffin and couldn't resist."

"Sarcophagus," I said. Not that the semantics mattered.

But... if we were going to talk murder, I may as well take advantage. "But how? How did the body get inside? Did any of you see anyone in here yesterday or Friday night who didn't belong?"

The women muttered amongst themselves.

"Of course not," Eliza said over the noise. "If we had, we would have thrown them out."

"Who had access to the lodge?" I asked.

"We opened the lodge at eleven AM yesterday," my mother said. "All the members had access after that point."

"You can hardly think one of us did it?" Eliza said, her nostrils pinching.

"No, no." I adjusted the collar of my navy hoodie. Was it getting warm in here? "Of course not. The killer was likely someone connected to Mr. Myatt. Were there any visitors to the lodge yesterday?"

"Only your museum team, I'm afraid," Cora said. "And the caterer, of course, but I include him in your team."

"That's not entirely true," Eliza said. "That group from Town Hall was here."

"What?" I asked. "What group?"

"The new mayor and some department heads," Eliza said, preening.

"What were they doing here?" I asked.

"Getting a private tour of the exhibits," Eliza said. "That woman said it was okay."

"What woman?" I asked.

"Your new registrar," my mother whispered in my ear.

I frowned. Chelsea hadn't mentioned a private pre-opening tour. Not that I minded. *Who you pay or who you know...* "Do you remember which department heads?"

"Parks and rec, permitting, business licenses, library services, and building inspection," Eliza said promptly. "Since my Berend became a town councilman, I've become *much* better acquainted with our public servants."

Since her son Berend was dating my friend Harper, I didn't comment. My mother, however, had no such qualms.

"Did you suggest the private tour?" my mother asked sharply. "If you thought that would buy Berend political points—"

"Nothing so crass." Eliza sniffed. "I was simply lunching with the mayor and the department heads yesterday." She brushed off the cuffs of her blue suit. "I mentioned the exhibit had been set up in record time this morning. Since she wasn't going to be able to attend the soft opening, I invited the mayor to preview the exhibit. For the museum's sake."

My mother's cornflower eyes narrowed.

"Hold on," I said. "I thought Ira Myatt was the head of the inspection department."

A teacup clattered against its saucer. Beside the samovar, a plump, gray-haired lady flushed. She hurried to her chair with her tea.

Eliza glowered at the woman. "He was," she said. "Mark Spicer and Ronnie Batson have been acting heads since Ira, er, left. They're both jockeying for the position. Now that Ira's definitely gone, I suppose one of them will get the job."

"So they were both at your, er, preview?" I asked.

"That's what I said, didn't I?" Eliza snapped. "Them and your registrar. She was fiddling with the exhibits when we all got here."

Fiddling? It was probably nothing. Chelsea was responsible for the exhibits. She had every right to fiddle until they burned. "Does anyone here know anything about the victim that they can add?" I asked.

Occasionally, vague questions got me surprisingly useful answers. I hoped it would work this time too.

Murmuring, the women looked at each other. One gray-haired woman wearing rhinestone spectacles raised her hand.

"Yes?" I asked.

"Ira had a very healthy appetite."

Okay. Not useful. "And you know this because...?"

"He ate lunch every Thursday at the Book Cellar," the woman said. "My Robert's the owner, you know," she added proudly.

I knew. The Book Cellar book and wine bar was right across the street from my old museum. I'd lunched there many a day.

At the thought, a gray weight clouded my chest. I wouldn't be able to dart across the street for a grilled cheese sandwich and glass of wine anymore.

I shook myself. The past hadn't been perfect. I needed to back off on the nostalgia. "Anyone else?" I asked hopefully.

No one responded.

"What time did the mayor and the others get their preview?" I asked.

"It was after lunch," Eliza said. "Around one."

I nodded. "And did you notice anything—"

"Of course not," she said. "If I had, I would have said something by now."

"Okay," I said. "I'm trying to develop a timeline of who was in the big hall—"

"Grand Hall," Cora corrected gently from the podium. A folding chair squeaked.

"The Grand Hall," I said, "and when."

"Aside from Chelsea," My mother said, "your team arrived Friday afternoon at two-o-clock. We left you alone until that caterer showed up. What time was that?"

"Five," I said. He'd wanted to see the final layout so he wouldn't be surprised the next evening. "Alex left with me and the rest of the museum staff at five-thirty. Did anyone go inside afterward that night?"

The women exchanged several shamefaced looks.

"Some of the lodge members might have taken a private tour as well," my mother said without a trace of shame. "But I believe we've already determined that none of us were involved."

We'd assumed it, because I couldn't imagine a gang of geriatric women offing a building inspector and stashing his body in their own lodge. If this crew wanted to get rid of someone, the body would never be found. I suppressed a shudder.

"And Saturday," I said, "no one had access until the lodge opened at eleven. What then?"

"A few of our members might have peeked into the Grand Hall," my mother said. "Chelsea arrived at noon—"

"Noon?" I asked, wrinkling my forehead. I wasn't used to keeping track of my employee's movements. I figured they knew their business. And if they achieved their goals, I didn't see the need to micromanage. Maybe that was a mistake.

My mother inclined her head, her squash-blossom earrings swaying. "She was concerned about some of the exhibits, she said."

"Did anyone go into the Grand Hall with her?" I asked.

"Why would we?" My mother raised a brow. "She knew her business. She left at approximately three-thirty. Your caterer arrived as she was leaving to begin his set-up. He really did a lovely job. The ghost-shaped ice sculpture was a nice touch. You arrived at four-thirty, which, if I may say, was cutting it rather close."

My mouth compressed. My timing had been fine. I'd just wanted to make sure there were no problems with the catering. The exhibit had already been set up. Besides, Alex had been in charge of putting out the tablecloths and napkins and such. All I'd had to do was set out some brochures and Paranormal History Museum stickers for the guests.

"So the caterer was alone until I arrived?" I confirmed.

My mother nodded.

"And Chelsea was alone too," I said. "What about the group from Town Hall? Were any of them left alone in the Grand Hall?"

"I wasn't paying attention to their comings and goings," Eliza said. "I was busy with the mayor. I suppose one of them *may* have lagged behind. But I would have noticed if they'd been carrying a mummy with them."

I'd have to ask Chelsea if she'd left them alone at any point. "How long were they here?" I asked.

"No more than thirty minutes," Eliza said. "Then everyone went their separate ways."

Leaving a period between one-thirty and three when only Chelsea was in the hall. "Could someone have snuck a body in here without anyone noticing?" I asked.

In the crowded room, the women exchanged uneasy glances. *Silly question*. Of course someone could have. I'd spent enough time at the lodge to know that the women congregated here, in the library, or in the upstairs offices.

Still, it would take a lot of nerve for someone to bring a body through the front door. But they might not have to.

"What about the back door from the parking lot that opens into the Grand Hall?" I asked. "I'm assuming that was locked."

My mother winced.

"What?" I asked.

Cora sighed, the folds of her velvet caftan rippling. "We've been having some problems with that door."

"What sort of problems?" I asked.

"It appears it might have been left open." Cora gripped the podium.

"Since when?" I asked.

"Since last year?"

"Last..." I swayed. The Grand Hall with my exhibits had been unlocked and unguarded? *Anyone* could have gotten in there.

chapter five

Spirit Cabinet

USA, *circa 1860*

The spirit cabinet illusion was pioneered by the Davenport brothers, two fraudulent mediums active during the height of the spiritualist movement in the 1850s and '60s. This box illusion involved the brothers seating themselves inside a custom-made wooden cabinet the size and shape of a wardrobe. Once inside, they were bound by audience members. And then the cabinet's doors were closed.

Now hidden from view, the brothers were able to free themselves and start the show. Musical instruments would be played by "the spirits." Objects, including pale, disembodied hands, would appear from holes in the cabinet as if from the aether. Their 19th century audiences, unused to magic acts, believed the spirits were at work. When the doors were finally opened, the brothers would be seated again, their hands and ankles tied.

Other mediums copied the Davenport brothers' act before their trick was exposed by an amateur magician in 1865. This cabinet is an example of such a copy.

It's amazing how friends in low places can speed the bureaucratic process along. And though I hated using the who-you-pay or who-you-know leverage, I was also feeling a little frantic about opening the museum.

I sat in my vintage pickup in the parking lot at Town Hall. Morning fog speckled the windshield with moisture. The dash clock ticked. I'd arrived twenty minutes before the scheduled meeting. My too-early arrival smacked of desperation.

To kill time, I thumbed through social media on my phone. I paused on a page of recent photos from the museum and groaned.

I'd had the bright idea of chronicling online every step in the process of opening the new museum. That had included posting photos of us setting up for the soft opening in the Ladies Aid hall. And *that* had included a picture of Leo making like a tomb painting in front of the sarcophagus.

I'd posted it Friday afternoon. Anyone following the museum would have known the sarcophagus was at Ladies Aid. They *wouldn't* have known the stupid door would be unlocked. But it could have given them time to plot and to plan how to rid themselves of an inconvenient body.

I studied the comments. Lots of thumbs up and mummy gags.

A mummy covered in chocolate and nuts has been discovered in the Ladies Aid Lodge. Archaeologists believe it may be Pharaoh Rocher.

"There's a dumb joke born every minute," I muttered and checked my watch. Now I was only ten minutes early. It would be five by the time I found the office I was supposed to go to. Prompt and professional, but not desperate.

My phone rang. It was a number I didn't recognize, but I answered anyway. "This is Maddie."

"Maddie Kosloski? This is Sandra Bennington from the San Francisco Times. I'm working on a story about the mummy found in your cursed coffin."

My stomach rolled. "Sarcophagus," I said weakly. "It's a sarcophagus." A detail I *really* needed to stop focusing on.

The term sarcophagus *did* commonly refer to a coffin. But in ancient Egypt, mummies were buried like Russian nesting dolls. They were wrapped in linens, laid in a coffin, and the coffin itself set inside a sarcophagus.

Most sarcophagi were made of stone. The museum's was not. It was a miracle it had survived the centuries.

She laughed lightly. "Right. Cursed sarcophagus. How did the body get in there?"

"The police investigation is ongoing, and I'm not a part of it. You should talk to Ja—Laurel Hammer. She's one of the detectives in charge." And she *hated* talking to reporters. *Ha.*

"What connection—?"

"Sorry," I said. "I've got to go."

Disconnecting, I stepped from my pickup, slid my phone into the back pocket of my jeans, and strode into Town Hall. It was a one-story, modernish building with a miniature vineyard in front for landscaping.

A nice lady at the front desk pointed me toward the permitting department. Soon I was seated in a windowed conference room overlooking a parking lot.

Three others sat around the table. The inspector from Sunday, Ronald, sat across from me. Opposite him was his rival for the top inspector position, Mark Spicer. At the end of the table sat a slender woman, Janice Walsh. She looked too young to be running the permitting department.

"You're right." Janice adjusted the sleeve of her caramel-colored suit jacket. Highlights wove through the woman's mid-length brown hair. "There is a rule that buildings that old are grandfathered in to ADA requirements."

Ha. I knew there was a solution. Folding my arms, I smiled triumphantly.

"The problem," she continued, "is you were supposed to file a form requesting the exemption."

My smile faltered. "No problem. I'll fill out the form."

"The deadline for your property was thirty days ago," Ronnie said. "You're too late."

What? Blood thumped in my ears. "I might not have been late if the inspection hadn't been delayed," I said hotly.

"Delayed? Ira was dead," Ronnie said. "Murdered. Put inside your coffin."

"Sarcoph—" Shame heated my face, followed immediately by shock. *Wait.* He didn't think *I'd* been involved in...?

My stomach plunged. But why *wouldn't* he think that? Ira had inspected my museum. He'd been found in my sarcophagus. And I'd had easy access to both the lodge and the sarcophagus.

Mark cleared his throat. He was a big, florid man with sandy hair and an easy smile. "I think we can agree no one here's at fault for... Ira. The question is, how do we move forward?"

Right. Move forward. We had to move forward. *Preferably before Halloween.*

"What do you think, Janice?" Mark asked the slight woman beside him.

Janice fiddled with her pen. "These are unusual circumstances. If Ira had made his inspection when he was supposed to, this would have been flagged at the time. It should have been flagged earlier, frankly." She sighed. "If you fill out the form now, I think we can move forward."

I sagged in my chair. *Thank you.* "Great. Do you have a copy?"

Janice smiled briefly and rose. "I'll go print one out." She walked from the room. The wooden door drifted shut behind her.

An awkward silence fell. I studied the men. They'd all been at the soft opening. Janice too. Had they seen anything suspicious?

"I'm sorry about your colleague," I finally said. "I can't imagine what a shock it must have been, seeing someone you knew fall out of that sarcophagus. And wrapped up like..." A *mummy.* I trailed off, embarrassed.

"It wasn't very funny." Mark clawed a hand through his straight, sandy hair.

"Neither was Ira," Ronnie said. "He would have hated the joke."

"What was he like?" I asked.

Ronnie shook his head. "Couldn't really tell you. His policy was the office was for work, not for making friends."

"Then what—?"

Janice strode into the conference room. She set a piece of paper on the wooden table in front of me. "Here you go. Fill it out now, and we're good."

I patted my empty pockets. "Ah... Have you got a—?"

Ronnie pulled a pen from the pocket of his button-up white shirt and handed it to me. "Here you go."

"Thanks." I bent to the form. Shockingly, it was short and simple. I signed with a flourish and slid it across the table to her. "What's next?"

"Next, we'll need to set an appointment for your next inspection based on this." Mark glanced at Janice. "We'll get back to you."

"It's just that our grand opening is scheduled for October 31st," I said, scalding anxiety pulsing in my chest. I *had* to make the grand opening. The invitations had already gone out.

Mark frowned. "Our schedule—"

The conference room door opened. Harper, in a fitted chocolate-colored suit and turtleneck strode into the room. She smiled. "I heard you were here, Maddie. How's everything going?"

"They've been really helpful," I gushed. "The paperwork's done. We're setting an appointment for the final inspection before our grand opening."

"That's great," Harper said. "I love to hear about government efficiency." She brushed her thick, dark hair over one shoulder.

"Yep," I said, eyeing the inspectors. "Everything's been cleared up."

"Everything," Harper said, "but why one of our inspectors wound up in your sarcophagus."

"Yeah," I said, uneasy. "That."

"Awful as this was, maybe finding his body in your sarcophagus is a good thing—for Ira, I mean." Her olive skin colored. "I just mean, now we know he's, ah, dead. And a detective was on the scene. Plus, with all the help you've given the police in the past... I'm sure Ira will get justice, one way or another."

The three bureaucrats turned to stare. I sank lower in my chair and smiled weakly.

I knew why Harper had said something so embarrassingly clichéd. I'd saved her from a kidnapper last year. She was still irrationally grateful. But now I sounded like the town busybody.

Mark cleared his throat. "Okay then. We'll call you about the next inspection."

We rose, and the others left Harper and me in the conference room.

She grimaced. "Sorry. I don't know why I said that about you. The staff here is so respectful to we town councilors—too respectful. I catch myself rambling on and trying too hard. I feel like a..."

"Like a fraud?" I was all-too familiar with imposter syndrome. I'd been living it since the museum had catapulted into the big leagues. Or maybe the middle leagues?

"Exactly." Her nose wrinkled. "Did it sound as bad as I think?"

I canted my head. "You *might* have sounded a little like a character on *Murder She Wrote.*"

"Terrific." She made a face.

"Hey," I said, "Jessica Fletcher kicked ass."

Harper gave a short laugh. "I did love that show." She checked her watch. "Want to grab lunch and eat our insecurities away?"

"That should go without saying." I followed her out the door and past an atrium lush with greenery. "How well *did* you know Ira?"

"Not that well," she said. "He had a reputation for honesty. In my interactions with him, he was tough—a little harsh, to be honest. But he was fair, and I respected him. Ira didn't deserve to die. And wrapping him up like a mummy..."

Harper stopped beside a potted ficus in the tiled lobby and turned to face me. "The sarcophagus, the wrappings—it made it seem like a sick joke. But Ira's dead. It's no joke. It's terrible. He was a town employee."

And odds were the answers to his murder lay inside Town Hall.

chapter six

ELIAS ASHMOLE'S THEATRUM CHEMICUM Brittannicum
England, 1652

Born in 17th century England, Ashmole was an astrologer, politician, and royal officer. His book on alchemy claimed to contain the secrets of turning lead into gold. The illustration you see open before you represents the Twelfth Gate, the final rite in the alchemical process. Though the material aspects of alchemy have been debunked, many claim it is truly an allegory for turning one's spiritual lead into gold, and the Chemicum was influential to later scientists, including Isaac Newton.

Humility might make angels of us all. But I don't know anyone who enjoys the process.

And I *really* hated being humbled when I was actually wrong.

"You can't keep an antique book like that on an unfinished wooden stand." Chelsea scowled and gestured toward the glassed-in display. A book with yellowing pages covered in black and white illustrations lay open beneath it.

"The chemicals will damage the cover," she continued. It may have been an effect of her Cleopatra eyeliner, but her expression was imperious.

Exhaling slowly, I reminded myself this was why I'd hired Chelsea. To bring in the expertise I didn't have. But did she have to be so indignant about my ignorance? "What sort of display do you suggest?"

"We'll need a hygrometer for starters."

My lips compressed. Oh, yeah. Right. A *Hygrometer*.

Beside me, Leo coughed. His black leather jacket was slung over one shoulder. Its folds half obscured his latest museum t-shirt, featuring a QR code.

The young woman rolled her eyes. "To measure the humidity inside the case."

I smiled bitterly. That actually sounded reasonable and necessary. But how much was it going to cost?

GD glowered from his perch on the freestanding wall and meowed. I shot the ebony cat a glance. I was glad he'd made himself comfortable in the new museum, but honestly. Did he have to take Chelsea's side?

At least Herb wasn't here. He'd been butting heads with the registrar since I'd hired her.

Chelsea's upper lip curled. "This is central California swamp land. Or it used to be. We'll likely need a dehumidifier as well. And not just for this book. For all the books you intend to display. Not that they *should* be displayed. These are so rare—"

"There's no point in having these exhibits if people can't see them." My tone was tarter than I'd intended, and my mouth compressed. We'd gone around on this before.

Granted, Chelsea knew more than me about preservation. What she really seemed to want was to hide everything away in a sterile environment. But the point of this collection was for the public to be able to enjoy it. Safely.

She tossed her smooth, near-black hair. "I'll see about that hygrometer." She stomped down the charcoal-painted hallway.

Leo clapped my shoulder. "You sure you want to keep her around?"

I sighed. "I'm sure she's right about the book. This isn't exactly a dry environment."

It was amazing the books had survived as well as they had under their old owner. He'd kept them in a warehouse that was hygrometer free. "How much do hygrometers cost anyway?" I burst out.

"Fifteen bucks online."

I blinked. That wasn't bad. True, we'd likely need more than one, but still... "How do you know?"

He shrugged. "Chelsea's been ranting about hygrometers for the last three weeks. I had to look up what they were."

"Three *weeks*? Why is this the first I've heard about them?" Unless someone had told me and I'd forgotten—another sign I was in over my head. I swallowed.

"You've been busy with the soft opening." He shrugged. "And now...? Learn anything about the dead guy?"

Was I that predictable? "I'm not being nosy. Well, okay, I am. But... He was put in our sarcophagus like some sort of joke. I can't just ignore it."

He pulled the jacket off his shoulder and folded it over one arm. "I get it. It pisses me off too. Just because we're a paranormal museum, it doesn't mean we're a body dump."

"It's more than that." I shook my head. "And no, I haven't learned much. I let the world know there was a sarcophagus at Ladies Aid that night when I posted it on social media. And the lock wasn't working on the back door, so anyone could have gotten inside that hall."

"I don't suppose the lodge has any security cameras?"

"Of course not." I turned and walked down the narrow hallway toward the exit. "They're working on the assumption no one would dare infiltrate their *sanctum sanctorum.*"

"Huh?"

"Inner sanctum."

"I suppose late night would have been the best time for dumping a body," Leo said. "The town's dead after midnight. But how would they know they could get in?"

We walked past the Zoltan fortune telling machine. The turbaned mannequin inside studied us with dead eyes.

"I don't know," I said. "Maybe someone discovered they could get in when we were setting up on Friday, had a spare body on their hands, and went back for it?" It seemed like a lot though. "But how else could you sneak a body in under everyone's nose?"

"Not everyone," Leo said. "The ladies were pretty good about not going in there when I was working."

"They admitted going in and out when they thought the place was empty though," I said. "Whoever put that body in the sarcophagus was taking a big risk."

"The killer must have been desperate," Leo said.

I shot him a surprised look. "I suppose you're right. If sneaking the body into the lodge was a safer bet than keeping it where it was..." Where *had* the body been kept? It hadn't looked like it had been lying around for weeks. It certainly hadn't smelled like it. Maybe he'd been killed more recently?

And maybe I needed to focus on museum business. "Have you seen Herb?" I asked.

"He's been holed up in his office all morning. Door closed."

My chin dipped. "Huh." If Herb didn't want to be disturbed, I wouldn't poke the emaciated little bear. Especially since I didn't have the answer he wanted on his curation course.

We emerged into the gift shop. At the front of the building, windows overlooked a parking lot. It wasn't the best view, so I'd recently installed semi-sheer blinds to allow in light. They had the added bonus of creating spooky silhouettes of everyone who walked past.

Round tables with neatly stacked hoodies and t-shirts dotted the space. Books on the paranormal lined the shelves. One wall was devoted to divination, with displays of Tarot cards, spirit boards, and pendulums.

At the counter were the postcards and stickers and bookmarks—impulse purchases. At least I hoped people would be impulsive and buy them. The museum might now be a non-profit, but we still had to pay our employees. And me.

The glass exit door opened. A tanned, middle-aged woman with shoulder-length, frosted hair teetered inside on lime green sandals. The odor of cigarettes wafted off her hot-pink parka and thick wooly scarf. The get-up seemed extreme since it was over seventy degrees out.

I sucked in my cheeks. *Dammit.* I shouldn't have left that door unlocked. "Sorry," I said. "We're not open yet."

"I'm not a tourist," she graveled. "I'm here about the coffin."

"Ah..." I glanced at Leo. "Coffin?"

"That Egyptian coffin where Ira was stuck," she said. "I read it happened in the museum. So where is it?" She glanced around the gift shop.

"Sorry," I said, "who are you?"

"Day. Sidney Day."

Leo and I stared dumbly at her.

"Ira's ex," she continued. "Wife. Ex wife. I just flew in. I came straight here."

Flew in? My heart sank. Ex-wives usually made the best suspects, but it sounded like she might *not* be one. "Flew in from...?"

"Palmetto, Florida. Well, via St. Petersburg. There's no airport in Palmetto. So where is it?"

That was that then. Not a suspect, not a witness. *If* she was telling the truth. "Have you spoken with the police yet?" I asked.

"Over the phone," she said. "Some detective named Hammer called me."

"Does she know you're here?" I asked, wary. Laurel would have my guts for garters if she thought I was interviewing her witnesses before she got a chance.

"No." She plucked a postcard of a spirit photograph from the rack by the brass register. "Why should they? It's none of the cops' business where I am."

Oh, boy. The prudent thing to do would be to say as little as possible and move her along. "It's just that the police confiscated the sarcophagus," I said.

"The what?" she asked blankly.

"The Egyptian coffin thing," Leo supplied.

"Oh." She returned the postcard, nicking its edge on the wire rack. "Why not just say that?"

"I'm sorry for your loss," I said, in a vain attempt to regain control of the conversation.

"Why? You didn't know Ira, and you don't know me."

"How do you know I didn't know him?" I asked.

She sneered. "You're too old."

My mouth pinched. I'd just turned thirty-five. That was hardly *old.*

"Ira liked 'em younger." She pulled another postcard from the rack and squinted at it. "It's why I kicked him to the curb."

I tilted my head. "He was cheating on you?" I winced. So much for saying as little as possible and moving her along. But did Jason know Ira was a player? Jason would as soon as she got to the station. I needed to stop talking and let her go.

"Ira was cheating like a Russian gymnast," she said. "Though not cheating *with* any gymnasts I know of. That was an analogy. I caught him with that girl from his office."

Could Ira have been killed by a jealous lover? I struggled briefly with myself. *Don't do it.* "Which girl?" I asked.

She braced her elbow on the brass cash register. "Does it matter?"

"It might to the police," I said.

"I already talked to them on the phone. *Did he have any friends?* No. His whole life was work. *Did he have any enemies?* Duh. *Someone* killed him. I mean, what kind of dumb question was that?"

I relaxed. So they'd already interviewed her. I wasn't interfering in their investigation after all.

"So you flew all the way out here to see the sarcophagus?" Leo asked.

"No, I came to collect Ira's personal effects." She straightened off the antique register and gestured expansively. "I've got rights you know. Now that the alimony's gone, I've got to take care of myself."

Leo and I nodded like robots. She was fantastic, a caricature of a trashy widow. I was a little mesmerized.

"Why, ah, did you want to see the sarcophagus anyway?" It seemed a little ghoulish.

Her lips curved upward, displaying flecks of red lipstick on her teeth. "I wanted to see his final resting place. But I guess it's not that final, huh? The cops got him now."

She flicked the postcard to the glass counter. "Well, if you got nothing for me, I'm off like a prom dress." Pivoting on her lime-green heels, she sashayed out the door.

"Wow," Leo said.

Wow indeed. "Let that be a warning, young man. Choose your girl-friends wisely."

So Ira had been a player. And his taste in women ran to the… erratic. My breath hitched. Had his love life gotten him killed? I shook my head. I was speculating. I needed to focus on who had access to the lodge, like my caterer.

I strode past the ticket booth, hesitated outside Herb's closed door, and walked inside my office. Dropping into my executive chair, I opened my laptop and studied my calendar. The to-do list was long.

Ignoring it, I opened a web browser and typed in Alex Cookson's name. Only one article appeared, from the San Benedetto Times. I clicked on it.

COOKSON CATERING COMES TO SAN BENEDETTO

I was fortunate to attend the grand opening and ribbon cutting for Cookson Catering in San Benedetto. At least a hundred people came out to support the owner and chef, Alex Cookson. And town councilwoman Harper Caldarelli assisted with the ribbon cutting.

Cookson Catering can be utilized for all kinds of events, such as bridal showers, business meetings, grand openings, weddings, and private din-ners.

I studied the photo of Harper and Alex holding an oversized pair of scissors and cutting a yellow ribbon in front of the catering company's glass door. Wynnona stood beside her husband, her head turned to the side.

I followed her gaze and frowned. She was looking at Ira Myatt.

What had the building inspector been doing at their grand opening? But maybe it wasn't strange. She'd said they were friends. And depart-ment heads had come to the museum's soft opening, after all.

Or maybe there was something more.

Fridays were our usual girls' night out for Harper, Adele and me. But we'd agreed that circumstances required an earlier after-work meet-up at the microbrewery.

In a booth beside a glittering copper vat, we talked about Adele's tearoom expansion and the new museum.

"I don't know what you're worried about." Adele sipped her beer. The reddish light from the stained glass lamp tinted her hair, done up in a loose chignon. Her pink suit jacket was unbuttoned—Adele's version of loosening up.

"You've always been an ace marketer," my friend continued. "You did wonders with the first little museum. And you say your new collection is world class. It'll be fine."

"I appreciate your confidence," I said. "But there are a lot more moving parts now. And with this body..."

Adele made a sympathetic face. "Has it set you back?"

"No," I said explosively. "It's been great publicity. And *that* makes me feel like garbage."

"You can't help that." Harper shifted in the booth. She wore a rich brown turtleneck, so dark her smooth, long hair nearly faded into it. "And I'm sure you're not taking advantage."

"I'm not. Or I'm trying not to." I fiddled with the damp beer mat. "Do you remember Alex Cookson's grand opening?" I asked Harper. "For his catering company?"

"Yeah. Great food."

"Ira was there," I said.

"We like to encourage the staff to see the results of their work," Harper said.

"So it was normal for him to be there?" I asked.

Harper brushed back her hair. "Totally. Why?"

"She thinks her caterer is a suspect," Adele supplied.

"No," I said quickly. "I mean, yeah, I guess he is. He knew Ira. He was at the soft opening. But that doesn't mean he's a killer. I'm just exploring all options."

"Such as?" Harper asked.

"Ira's coworkers were at the soft opening too," I said, "including Janice and his two rivals for chief inspector."

She stiffened. "Just because they were at the soft opening, it doesn't mean they put his body in that sarcophagus. In fact, it sort of reasons against it."

I wasn't sure about that, but I didn't want to argue. "It could have been someone else he'd inspected and given a bad mark to."

Harper's dark brows rose. "When Ira disappeared, other inspectors came in to review his work. *They* weren't killed."

Thank you, devil's advocate. But she wasn't wrong.

And that was the nice thing about friends. They could tell you what they thought, even if you didn't really want to hear it. I was glad, at least, that this one thing—our friendship—hadn't changed.

"All right," I said. "Well, Ira's ex-wife said he liked younger women."

Harper studied the tin ceiling. "Hm. You think an angry boyfriend or husband came after him?"

"Have you heard Ira was a player?" Adele asked her.

"No," she said. "So I've got no suspects to offer. But it's not the sort of gossip the staff would share with me."

We continued hashing out the murder. But my friends couldn't provide any more intel than I'd already gleaned.

After we left the microbrewery, instead of driving home, I returned to the new museum. I told myself it was to check on GD. But I liked having the new museum to myself.

Unlocking the front door, I stepped inside. I'd turned the lights off when I'd left. But the moonlight streaming through the blinds was enough to navigate by. I made my way past the ticket booth into the foyer. An expanse of darkness stretched before me.

But a bubble of excitement swelled in my chest. I still couldn't quite believe the new museum existed. As much as I'd loved my old museum, it had been a little cramped. Okay, a lot cramped. And though we'd had a decent collection of spiritualist objects, the new museum was a whole other level.

We had art. Valuable, beautiful art. This was an interactive museum now, not just a roadside attraction. And it felt magical.

I moved toward a light switch. My feet skidded from under me, and I was airborne. I gasped, and my back slammed onto the floor.

Too stunned to do more, I wheezed. Fortunately, I'd tucked my head at the last minute so at least I hadn't bounced my skull off the linoleum. But everything else hurt.

Slowly, I rolled to my hands and knees. My left leg skidded backward, and I pancaked onto my stomach. Swearing, I levered myself up. My hands slipped forward.

What the hell? The floor was as slick as if it had just been waxed. And I *knew* I hadn't done that.

Something clanked inside the museum.

Heart thumping, I raised my head.

There was a thud, and then faint, masculine laughter.

I froze. Someone was in the museum.

chapter seven

PROMOTIONAL PHOTO OF ISRAEL *Regardie*

United States, 1942

Francis Israel Regardie (November 17, 1907 – March 10, 1985) was a British-American occultist, ceremonial magician, and writer. He is perhaps most famous for breaking his oath of secrecy to the magical society, The Hermetic Order of the Golden Dawn, to publish detailed books on their rituals and beliefs in order to preserve their magical knowledge after the society collapsed. In total, he published fifteen books on mysticism and the occult.

Someone was in the museum, and my heart hammered against my chest.

Someone was in the museum, and it wasn't Leo. My assistant would have turned the lights on.

Which meant someone had broken in. My knees wobbled. I was briefly glad I was already on the floor, slick and cool beneath my hands.

A masculine voice whispered up the stairs, and I tried to quiet my breathing. Did they know I was here? Had they heard my fall?

Because I'm *not* one of those women who laughs maniacally in the face of danger, I slipped my phone from my pocket and texted Jason.

Someone broke into the museum. I'm inside.

I hate texting. My fingers are always hitting the wrong keys. But I'm also not one of those women who have loud phone conversations while bad guys lurk nearby.

A text pinged loudly in response, and I winced.

Get out now.

My mouth tightened. Excellent advice. Wouldn't have thought of it myself.

I rolled to my side and attempted to get a foot under me. But I skidded like a cartoon coyote. Whatever had slicked up the floor seemed everywhere. Finally, I resorted to rolling my way toward the front door.

A childish voice floated up the stairs. "Dude, check it out."

I raised my head. A rush of heat flooded my skull. I *knew* that voice.

Kids. I rolled back toward the stairs. Pivoting onto my butt, I sat up and put a tentative foot on the nearest step. It was as slippery as the lobby.

I grasped the metal railing with both hands. Hanging from it, I eased myself down the steps. I touched bottom, and my sneakered feet found purchase. Carefully, I stood.

I took a few tentative steps. It seemed I was in the clear. I moved more swiftly toward the sounds of laughter through the dark warren of exhibits.

Pulling my cellphone from the pocket of my hoodie, I rounded a corner and switched on the phone's light. "Hey!"

Three pre-teen boys jerked away from the wall and spun to face me. Their eyes widened. They darted down the hall toward the back of the museum.

I lunged and caught the sweatshirt of the nearest—Jordan Hjelm. He writhed, his sweatshirt stretching, forcing my fingers to open slightly. But I clung on. "How much trouble do you want to be in, Jordan?"

He stopped struggling and turned, blue eyes wide. His blond hair was in the spiky style popular with the younger set. It made him look petrified. "M—Ms. Kosloski."

"Yeah. What are—?" My flashlight scanned the photos of twentieth-century occultists. Dion Fortune, Israel Regardie, Aleister Crowley... I sucked in a breath.

The framed photograph of a gentleman with a domed forehead, a shadow artfully hiding what may or may not have been a bald spot, now sported black-ink eyeglasses and half an oversized mustache.

"At least you kept the black and white theme," I muttered and let him go.

Jordan looked toward the hallway where his companions had fled.

"I'm calling your father regardless," I said. "There's nowhere to run."

His thin shoulders slumped. "It was just a joke."

"A joke? If the police had caught you—" I started and swore. *The police.* Hastily I texted Jason. *False alarm. Sorry. Everything's okay.*

"Is that my Dad?" he asked, expression pleading.

"No. The police." I flipped on the light switch, illuminating my secret society exhibit.

His narrow face whitened. "What?"

"Don't worry. I canceled the call." I phoned Mason.

"Who's that?" Jordan asked.

"Your dad."

"Wait, no—"

"Maddie?" Mason answered. "What's up?"

"I'm at the museum."

Jordan shook his head violently. He clasped his hands together in a prayerful gesture.

"With your son," I finished.

"Augh." Jordan crumpled forward and buried his blond head in his hands.

I stared, unmoved. Here's the thing. My parents didn't let me get away with *anything.* So I had no compunction about narcing on Jordan. It was for his own good.

Plus, my spine felt like someone had taken a hammer to it. I didn't know what they'd done to my floor or why, but they deserved what was coming.

"What's Jordan doing at your museum?" Mason asked.

"Minor vandalism."

"What?" he roared. I winced, jerking the phone from my ear.

"At least it had better be minor," I said to Jordan clapping my hand over the phone's mic. "What else did you do?"

"The picture's all," he said frantically. "Really."

"It's *not* all. What'd you do to the floor in the lobby?"

"What? Nothing. We just wanted to see the museum at night, when it was closed. And then we saw that weird guy, and—the ink's on the glass, not the photo. You can clean it off."

I put the phone to my ear. "He broke in with some friends. Alas, the others escaped my clutches."

"I'll be right there," Mason growled and disconnected.

I pocketed the phone. "How'd you get inside?"

He looked away, his expression sullen.

"Look," I said, "you've been caught, fair and square. Be happy it was me and not the cops, and take the L. Now, how'd you get in?"

"Through the air conditioning vent."

Vent? We didn't have any open vents. "Show me."

Sneakers dragging, he led me through the maze of exhibits and paused in front of the door to the storage room.

"Lead the way." I prodded him.

Jordan slouched inside. We walked down aisles of metal shelves laden with artifacts and neatly labeled boxes. He stopped in front of a wall with a gaping rectangular hole at eye level. A parking lot light gleamed outside.

My mouth puckered. I stared at the hole. "Where's the air conditioner?"

"Um. Still outside, I guess."

I stuck my head through the gap. Sure enough, the A/C was lying on the pavement, its electric cord snaking across a parking spot.

I withdrew and rubbed my forehead. The air conditioner was at least forty years old, and it was broken. Since this was only a storage room, I hadn't bothered to replace it. I'd just left it as filler for the wall. I hadn't realized someone could pull it out and get inside.

And I'd deal with that later. "All right. Come on." I led him to another shelf with cleaning supplies and grabbed a rag and window cleaner.

Maybe Jordan was telling the truth about not touching the floor. If they'd come in from the back, they'd have had access to cleaning supplies to slick the floor. But I'd caught them mid-museum. They might not have gotten to the foyer, at the front yet.

And I wanted to believe Mason's son was just a prankster, not a liar.

We made our way back to the black-framed photo. I plucked it from the wall and handed it to him. "Get busy."

The ink was surprisingly resistant. While Jordan scrubbed the glass, I talked.

"That weird guy you defaced was Paul Foster Case, one of America's most famous occultists and founder of the Builders of the Adytum, a mail order secret society."

He huffed a laugh. "Mail order?"

"I think it's kind of charming." I missed the days when getting a thick envelope full of paper was a thrill. "I suppose the society eventually will be moving online, if it hasn't already. It would save printing and postage."

"Whatever." He shrugged.

I smiled bitterly. But I couldn't expect everyone to get excited about twentieth century occultists. But since we were stuck together until Mason came to retrieve him, I plowed onward.

"Case modeled his society on the teachings of the Hermetic Order of the Golden Dawn. That was founded in 1906 by MacGregor Mathers after the original Golden Dawn folded in 1903. Petty bickering killed the first one, culminating in a magical duel between Mathers and Aleister Crowley."

He looked up from the smeary photo. "Magical duel?"

Ha. I *thought* that might interest him. "Mathers sent an astral vampire to attack Crowley. Crowley retaliated by siccing an army of demons led by Beelzebub on Mathers."

His blond eyebrows drew downward. "But... That's just dumb. None of that's real."

Ah, the arrogance of youth. "It was real to Crowley and Mathers. That said, the London lodge took your attitude. They expelled them both. The poet William Butler Yeats tried to keep the original Golden Dawn going, but the society fell apart not long after. I think everyone was too embarrassed to go on."

Jordan looked down at the photo in his hands. "And this guy was part of it?"

I nodded. "Part of the chain. Foster Case was downstream, picking up the magical philosophies and sort of Americanizing them. Mail order was a big part of that. I mean, how's an occultist in Topeka supposed to get to a lodge meeting in New York? Especially in the early 20th century. It was a lot harder to get around the country then, and they didn't have online meetings."

Jordan gave the glass another swipe.

"Things used to be a lot more mysterious," I said mournfully, then shook myself. "Although there's still plenty of mystery now. I think we just talk about weird things more today, and that makes it *seem* less mysterious."

"Maddie?" Jason called. He cursed, and there was a thud.

Briefly, I closed my eyes. "Here," I hollered. "Are you okay? The lobby's a little, ah, slick."

"Where are you?" he shouted.

"Come on," I told Jordan. "We're coming to you," I called.

"We?" Jason asked.

"Coming." I led Jordan down the twisting corridors and to the base of the lobby steps.

Jason clung to the ledge. "What the hell?"

Guiltily, I pressed my hand to my cheek. "Are you okay? I don't know why it's so slippery. One of the contractors must have..." *What?* Buffed and waxed the floor? When did *that* ever happen? And why did I believe Jordan was telling the truth?

I smothered a sigh. The answer to that was more of my own guilt. But it wasn't my fault Jordan's mother had committed a crime, only that she'd gotten caught. "Some kids broke in. I've called Jordan's father."

"I'll stop him from coming inside the front," Jason said. "We'll meet you at the back."

"Thanks."

Jordan and I retraced our steps, making our way to the rear door. When I opened it, two pairs of angry male eyes glared in.

"You broke into the museum?" Mason asked, his voice tight.

"We didn't actually *break* anything," Jordan said weakly.

"There's no real damage," I said quickly. I didn't want him adopting his mother's life of crime, but under the circumstances, I didn't want to go too hard on the kid either. "But I'd prefer it didn't happen again."

"It won't." Mason gripped his son's shoulder and steered him toward a waiting Dodge Charger. "I'll call you," he threw over his shoulder, and I nodded.

I winced. "Did you hurt yourself?" I asked Jason.

"No. I know how to take a fall."

"I wish you'd teach me." I massaged my lower back.

"Are you hurt?" His hand went to my waist.

"Just a little bruised."

His mouth compressed. "Who waxed that floor?"

"No idea. Jordan said he and his friends didn't—"

"Really?" Jason raised a dark brow. "And you believed him?"

"I found them at the back of the museum. He said they hadn't gotten any farther."

Jason shook his head. "It wouldn't be the first time someone from that family put you in danger."

"You can't blame Jordan for his mother."

"I wasn't referring to his mother."

My face warmed. "Oh." When Jordan's mother had gone missing, I'd helped Mason try to find her. It hadn't ended well.

That hadn't been Mason's fault. He couldn't have known what would happen. But when you're dating a cop, they tend to take a dim view of civilians playing detective.

"You need to fix that floor," he continued, "before someone does hurt themselves."

I rubbed the back of my aching neck. *Too late.*

chapter eight

PARAFFIN SPIRIT HAND

France, circa 1920

This waxen hand was part of a collection of hands that allegedly "apport-ed" into Polish medium Franek Kluski's seances. Franek Kluski, aka Teofil Modrzejewski (1873-1943), would set a bowl of hot paraffin in the room for "spirits" to dip their hands into. Houdini later exposed Franek as a fraud.

As much as I would have loved to have spent the rest of the evening with Jason, he was on duty. So we parted with promises to see each other tomorrow.

I *also* would have loved for one of the workmen to have admitted they'd spilled something in the lobby. But the next day, none did.

Dieter's brow sketched upward. "You think one of *my* guys waxed your floor? Seriously?" His paint-stained jeans sagged alarmingly. He scratched his chest through his paint-spattered tee.

A drill whirred from the back of the museum, and I winced. One of his workers was covering the hole where the A/C had once been with plywood. It was a temporary fix, but temporary was all they could manage right now.

"Or maybe they spilled something..." I trailed off, feeling foolish. I'd mopped the floor in the daylight. The entire floor had been slick—there hadn't been a spill.

So why was I bothering? Jordan had lied to get himself out of more trouble. I needed to move on. And yet, the Mystery of the Slippery Lobby nagged at me.

I shifted my weight. "Anyway, thanks for getting someone here so quickly. I know you're busy."

Since Dieter had upgraded from handyman to full-time contractor, he'd been in high demand. It was a miracle he'd been able to get here at all this morning. There was a lot of new construction happening in sleepy San Benedetto. I was happy for Dieter but not about all the transformations.

And yes, I *know* life is change. But I hoped the changes to my home-town were gradual and would fit our sleepy aesthetic. I hated the re-move-and-replace trend in the nearby Bay Area. The Bay was going from charming bedroom communities to high-density housing in the wink of a cynical eye. Driving there was torture.

"No prob, Mad Dog." Dieter grinned, and I flinched. He *knew* I hated that nickname. "If we don't get this done," he continued, "you'll only have more kids in your museum tonight. You know they're at school pounding their chests about their exploit this morning."

I laughed. "Is that what you would have done?"

His grin broadened. "No, I would have been the kid who tried it the next night and got caught."

Jason stuck his head into the lobby. "Is it safe?"

"The floor's clear." I motioned him inside, and he stepped into the elevated lobby. He wore his typical detective uniform—a navy suit and tie. And the uniform did for him what uniforms did for men every-where—made him look even hotter.

The two men traded grips and greetings. Dieter vanished down the stairs into the exhibits to collect his worker.

"You have time for a cup of coffee?" Jason asked.

I smiled, my heart growing lighter. "For you? Always."

We ambled down the street to the Sunshine Cafe, a diner with a 1950s vibe.

"How's your back?" Jason opened the door for me.

I preceded him into the restaurant. "A little sore, but I'll survive."

Jason nodded to a waitress and led me to a blue vinyl booth. We ordered coffee from the blue uniformed waitress, and she swished away.

"How's your investigation going?" he asked.

"It's—" My mouth pinched. "My investigation?"

He sighed. "Interviewing suspects at Town Hall?"

"Oh. I wouldn't exactly call it *interviewing*. I had to finish up the paperwork to grandfather in my building. Asking the inspectors about Ira was only polite."

"Mm, hm," he said, shooting me a skeptical look. "Your polite conversation got back to Laurel."

I sank lower on the blue seat. "Oh."

"You've been helpful in the past, and I appreciate it. And I've given up on trying to make you stop. But all of Town Hall knows you're asking about the murders. And they know what you've done in the past for Harper. This isn't good."

He was right, and my insides tightened. This was the line we always walked, because they were *his* questions to ask. "Jason, I—"

The waitress appeared with our coffee. "Can I get you anything else?"

"Not right now," Jason said. "Thanks."

She nodded and zoomed toward the kitchen.

"I'm sorry." I grabbed several sugar packets, ripped off their tops, and dumped them into my coffee. "I really didn't intend..." To what? To cause him problems? For it to have come off as an interrogation? Either explanation sounded lame.

"I'm sorry," I repeated. "But I *am* worried. The body was in my sarcophagus at my mother's lodge. I realize not everything's about me, but this seems personal. And in fairness, everyone's talking about Ira. It's all just so strange. I mean, where has Ira been all this time?"

"Dead."

I blinked. "What?"

"It looks like he was frozen. We can't tell for how long, but I'm guessing he was killed the day he went missing and has been in deep freeze ever since." He sipped his coffee.

"That... explains the dampness around the sarcophagus." He'd been defrosting. *Ew.* I cleared my throat. "So his ex could have killed him, but could she have put him in the sarcophagus?"

He shook his head. "She was in Florida when that sarcophagus was at Ladies Aid."

And the body definitely hadn't been in the sarcophagus before we'd brought it to their Grand Hall. "Speaking of the sarcophagus, should I be concerned about water damage?"

He raised his hand. "Someone in Town Hall put in a word for you with Sacramento. Your registrar has permission to observe the forensics team, but *only* observe."

I relaxed back in the booth and released a slow exhalation. *Thank you, Harper.* And I was willing to bet Jason had put in a word too. "That's good news. Thanks."

"I had nothing to do with it."

My stomach sank. He hadn't? "Well, thanks for putting up with my panic about that sarcophagus." Grabbing the metal tin of cream, I dumped that into my coffee too. Milky clouds billowed from its depths.

He shrugged. "The techs will be going over the sarcophagus tomorrow. I'll text you the address."

I grimaced. "Does this mean the sarcophagus has already been transported to Sacramento?"

Jason nodded, and I bit back a curse. Chelsea was not going to be happy about that. I wasn't thrilled either. Who knew what damage the move might have caused?

But the sarcophagus was in Sacramento now, and there was nothing I could do about it. The bell above the diner's front door jangled.

"Jason..." I turned the warm, white mug in my hands. "Do you think...? Could someone have slicked up the museum lobby as sabotage?" *Or to send me a warning?* "Someone could have been hurt."

Jason sipped his black coffee. "It had to have been the kids. Unless Dieter admitted to it?"

"Of course not, but—"

"Maddie?" Mason asked from behind me.

I twisted in the booth. Clad in a black tee and jeans, Mason strode toward us. My heart simultaneously squeezed and pounded harder, and not just because I was worried he'd overheard us.

Being a single parent was a challenge. But being a single dad because your baby mama had basically abandoned her kid... I couldn't even imagine.

Sure, it happened to others. But this was someone I knew, someone who was learning how to navigate fatherhood and a troubled pre-teen. And I'd played no small part in his ex's troubles with the law.

Mason stopped beside our table. "Hey," he said to Jason.

Jason nodded.

"I wanted to apologize again for my son," Mason told me.

I shook my head. "In a way the boys did me a favor. Now I know there's a secret entry to the museum to deal with."

"Don't tell Jordan that," Mason said. "I don't want him to have any room for excuses. He broke in. Period." He hesitated. "I tried to get the names of the other kids out of him. He wouldn't tell me."

"Irritating," I said. "But on the bright side, he's not a narc."

Jason sighed. Narcs made his job a lot easier. I nudged his foot with my own and smiled.

One corner of Mason's mouth lifted. "Small favors. But if the museum hadn't belonged to you, he might have been arrested. I've grounded him, but I'd like him to do some community service. At your museum, if you're up for it."

What? What was I going to do with a surly pre-teen? "Ah... The museum's not even open yet." I pulled back against the booth and glanced at Jason. *Get me out of this.*

Jason sipped his coffee. "I think it's a good idea."

"You do?" So much for romantic telepathy.

"There are consequences to our actions." Jason's face was a block of marble, his gaze on Mason. "The sooner kids learn that, the better choices they make."

A muscle flickered in Mason's jaw. He drew a deep breath and slowly released it. "Right."

What was I going to do? I couldn't be responsible for the delinquency of a minor. Especially since a part of me felt that I already kind of *was* responsible for Jordan's troubles.

I forced a smile, my stomach twisting. "Sure," I said. What was the worst that could happen? A chill raced down my spine. Why the hell had I thought that? Everyone knew it was a curse. I swallowed. "Why not?"

chapter nine

HOUDINI, HARRY (ERIK WEISZ) *Water Torture Cell Poster*

New York, 1915.

This poster promoted Houdini's famous act, the "Chinese Water Torture Cell." He first performed it in Berlin on September 21, 1912.

Tragically, the act set off a chain of events leading to Houdini's death. While in the tank, a piece of equipment broke and injured his leg, but against his doctor's orders, the magician continued the tour. While resting his leg on a couch, he was visited by some students. One asked if it was true he had unusually strong abdominal muscles. Houdini confirmed it. Before the seated Houdini could brace himself or prepare, the student delivered several surprise punches to his abdomen. Days later, Houdini died of peritonitis from the blows.

Houdini, a campaigner against fraudulent mediums, promised to communicate to his wife from the spirit world if he could. He never did.

When in doubt, ask your mother. Or ask *my* mother. I wouldn't say she knows everything that went on in San Benedetto, but she knew near enough. It could be more than a little unnerving.

Afternoon sun at my back, I stood on the brick stoop of the Ladies Aid lodge and stared unenthusiastically at the brass doorknocker. Its all-seeing eye stared witheringly back. I lifted the knocker and let it drop with a thud.

After a few moments, my mother opened the door. The sleeves of her navy blouse were rolled to her elbows. "Why Maddie," she said coolly. "This is a surprise."

Unspoken was the adjective: *unpleasant*. It hung in the air between us, nevertheless.

"Is this a bad time?" I asked.

"No," she said, drawing the word out, and she gazed at me speculatively. "But I'm afraid you've caught me in the middle of an attempted coup."

I rubbed my cheek. "A what?"

She pivoted and vanished inside. Taking that for an invitation, I followed her into the spacious entryway. Women bustled about, expressions tense. Baffled, I followed my mother past the photos of Ladies Aid leaders.

My mother climbed the carpeted stairs, and I trotted after her. "Coup?" I asked.

"The lock on the door to the Grand Hall," she said. "Eliza has charged—with some merit—that a different president would have gotten it fixed sooner. If we had, a killer wouldn't have gotten inside to place that poor man's body in your sarcophagus."

"It's really the museum's sarcophagus," I said weakly. "Not mine." But why *hadn't* my mother gotten the door fixed? The lapse seemed out of character.

"A special election's been called," she said, terse. She rounded a corner at the top of the stairs.

"What does Cora have to say?" I asked. Cora was her co-president.

"It's not Cora's fault," she snapped.

I followed her into her office, with its wood-paneled walls. "I didn't say it was," I said mildly and dropped into the yellowish wingchair in front of her desk.

She turned to me and frowned. "Sorry. I'm a bit on edge."

"Why *didn't* that door get fixed though? Was it funding?"

"Of course not." She dropped into the swivel chair behind the wooden desk. "The fact is, according to our bylaws, only people on the executive committee, such as myself, are allowed to have keys to the lodge. But we're not always around to let people inside, and they do love congregating in the sitting room. So several of the older members liked having a secret way in. The lock wasn't *obviously* broken," she went on rapidly. "You had to jiggle it a certain way. It's really rather tricky. The door *seemed* secure."

But it hadn't been secure. And someone had brought a body inside. On the wall, a Tarot card figure in needlepoint beamed a *you-should-have-known-better* smile.

"We'll have a new lock installed soon," she continued. "Barn doors and horses though. And now *no one* is happy. People can't find their way in off hours, and... You understand."

"Can't you just change the bylaws?" I crossed my ankle over one knee.

"That requires a two-thirds majority, which we don't have."

"Does Eliza have a shot at retaking the presidency?" I remembered when she'd been in charge the last time. The vibe of the organization had turned rather grim.

My mother shrugged. "Finding a building inspector's corpse in our Grand Hall has shaken morale. It's not the body, you understand. We've all dealt with those. It's the murder and the break-in. It doesn't matter that Ira wasn't killed here. Discarding his body in our hall was a desecration."

"How do you know he wasn't killed here?"

She canted her head. "Obviously, he was frozen months ago and then brought to the lodge."

"Obviously?" I asked, peeved. I mean, yeah, *I'd* known he was frozen, but only because I'd heard from Jason. How had my mother learned about it?

"Martha Milhoun's grandnephew works for the Sacramento crime lab," she continued, by way of explanation.

Oh, well. If you can't beat 'em, etc., etc. I'd come to her for intel, after all. "Did her nephew tell you anything else?"

"*Grand*nephew. And no."

Drat. "I spoke with Ira's ex-wife," I said casually.

"Yes, I heard Sidney was in town."

How did she...? Augh. "She said Ira didn't have much of a social life." *Aside from his girlfriends.*

"Ira was a bit of a loner. So if you're looking for information on the man, I'm afraid I can't help you."

"No," I said, "but I was curious about his co-workers."

"It's common knowledge that Ronnie Batson and Mark Spicer are jockeying for Ira's old job. Just don't call him Ronnie to his face. He hates it."

Uh, oh. Had I called him Ronnie? I couldn't remember. And he was in charge of signing off on the final inspection. I swallowed. "Good to know. Anything else?"

"Ronnie's in an astrophotography club with Harriet's daughter."

I couldn't see how that connected to Ira's murder. And which Harriet? Harriet from the Historical Association? I didn't think she was in Ladies Aid.

My mother stared expectantly. "Well? Aren't you going to write that down? They meet tonight at the library."

Hastily, I grabbed a pen and yellow notepad off her desk and scribbled a note. "Astrophotography. Got it. But what would really be helpful is information on their relationships."

"Spicer is part of a cooperative gaming group that meets Sundays at the Sunshine Cafe."

"A gaming group?" I asked, nonplussed.

"You said you wanted relationship information. The group's cooperative."

"What does that mean?"

"It means they're playing together against the game, instead of playing against each other. Write it down."

I wrote it down. "Anything else?"

She tapped her chin. "Janice Walsh in permitting is a bit of a drinker."

I sat forward. Now we were getting somewhere. "How do you know?"

"She's a member of the Plot 42 Wine Club and never misses a chance for her free glass. She's there every Saturday."

"Seriously?" I pressed my lips together. Adele's parents owned the winery. *I* was a member of that wine club. It didn't make me an alcoholic. I wasn't there drinking every Saturday either, though.

"I *know*," she said, misunderstanding. "She's really abusing her membership privilege. If she keeps it up, they're going to stop giving free glasses to wine club members."

"Do you know about any conflicts between the people in Ira's department?" I asked.

"Really, how would I know that? I'm not the all-seeing eye."

My mouth compressed. *Tell that to whoever designed the Lodge's crest.*

"If I was," she continued, "I would have done something about that lock."

"Okay. Thanks." I rose. "I'll leave you to your campaign."

If my mother couldn't help me... I was going to an astrophotography meetup.

"Uranus!" A shot of the blue planet flashed onto the screen, and I suppressed a snicker.

And yes, I knew my reaction was childish. But *you* try sitting through a slideshow of blurry dots and swirls for an hour. It was worse than my mother's old vacation photos.

The astrophotography group met in the town library's basement. I hoped they'd gotten a deal on the room. It was as barren as the lunar photos I'd just suffered through.

"You can even see one of its irregular moons," Ronald muttered appreciatively.

There was a scattering of applause. The balding man behind the projector stepped to the wall and switched on the light. "Thanks, you guys. I'm really making progress, and it's largely due to your advice."

The others rose, clapping each other's backs and saying their goodbyes.

I wound through the dozen chairs to Don't-Call-Me-Ronnie, at the front. "Hi again, Ronald."

The lanky redhead folded the metal chair he'd been sitting in. "Oh, hi, Maddie. I didn't know you were interested in astrophotography."

Since everything I knew about it I'd learned at tonight's meeting, I grimaced. "I'm actually more interested in night-sky photography," I lied. "You know, getting images of the earth and sky together. But I thought I'd expand my knowledge and drop in, see what your group was up to."

"It's a good idea." Ronald walked to a metal dolly and stacked the folded chair beside the others. "Though you can't do much of night-sky photography in San Benedetto. Too much light pollution."

"I suppose you usually go into the Sierras for your pictures?" I asked. Only two hours away, it was the nearest spot where you could really see the stars.

He nodded. "You?"

"Oh. Yeah," I said. "The big trees and the Milky Way. And all those lakes..." How was I going to steer the conversation to Ira? "Do you ever do any photography at work?" I smothered a wince. What kind of question was that?

He gave me an odd look. "Uh, no astrophotography. No."

A woman brushed past holding a chair. Smiling, Ronnie took it from her and set it on the dolly with the others.

"It's just that I heard Ira was into photography," I ad-libbed.

"Was he? He didn't mention it. But he didn't talk much about his personal life."

"Yeah." I glanced away. "I heard that too." It was the first honest thing I'd said all night.

"His work was his life." Ronald's sunburnt forehead wrinkled. "At least, that's what we all thought."

"I heard he was a stickler for the rules."

"You kind of have to be if you're an inspector. That's the whole point."

"Yes, but not all of the people he inspected were happy about it," I guessed.

He chuckled. "Oh, yeah. I didn't think that cryonics place was ever going to get approved. Ira got so frustrated."

"*Ira* was frustrated?" He'd inspected my donor's business?

"Yeah. I mean, *cryonics*. None of us understood the equipment or environmental impacts involved. Mark and Ira had to do a ton of research to sort it out. Mark even took a special course." A worried expression crossed his narrow face. "Maybe I should have taken more courses," he muttered.

"Who knows? Maybe someone will want to install an observatory in San Benedetto," I joked. "You'll have the telescope angle covered."

"This town's too flat for an observatory. And the light pollution..." He rambled on about the necessary requirements for an observatory, and I settled in for a long bout of pretending to listen.

Finally, I escaped into the library parking lot and walked to my pickup. I frowned. Weird. Why did it seem so small...? I stopped short. The tires bagged on the pavement as if they'd melted.

How could both tires...? Dazed, I walked to the other side of the truck and gaped.

All four. Four dead tires. No wonder my pickup looked shorter. It *was* shorter.

Magma-level heat flushed from my chest to the top of my head. Four tires hadn't just gone flat. I didn't need to examine the gaping rubber to know someone had slashed my tires.

chapter ten

WATERCOLOR BY GEORGIANA HOUGHTON

1871, London

British medium Georgian Houghton (1814-1884) produced her first auto-matic spirit drawing during a séance in 1859. Her abstract, non-objective style predated that of abstract artists Kandinsky and Piet Mondrian, both of whom were influenced by the spiritualists. Houghton's work inspired British artist Austin Osman Spare and the Swedish artist Hilma af Klint.

My left eyelid twitched. It was *sweeping*. How hard was sweeping? Why had I agreed to let Jordan work off his crime in the museum?

The pre-teen pushed the broom awkwardly over the sawdust. This technique would have worked fine with a push broom, but he held a standard kitchen broom.

Not only had Jordan apparently never wielded a broom in his life, but he'd also never noticed his parents using one. And his mother worked as a hairdresser. They swept hair every day.

Was he trying to look helpless so he'd get out of the work? "Would you be open to a suggestion?" I asked, forcing my voice to stay level.

Scowling, he jerked back his arm. The end of the broom struck a storage shelf, and the bronze skull on it rattled.

I stepped away, my hands raised in surrender. Maybe he really *had* managed not to notice anyone IRL or on TV sweeping a floor. It would be mildly impressive if it weren't so irritating.

But he'd figure it out eventually. Maybe. I retreated from the storage room.

"Maddie." Chelsea strode down the aisle, lined with vintage photos of famous killers. The glowers in this murderers row had nothing on hers. "The sarcophagus is already in Sacramento," she said. "They were supposed to let *us* move it."

"Us moving it wasn't going to happen. They weren't going to let us take it out of the chain of evidence."

She jammed her hands on the hips of her little black skirt. "Who *knows* what damage they've done?"

I rubbed my arms. She wasn't wrong. I didn't see how I could have stopped the cops, but what if there *had* been a way? "We'll work around it."

"Work around it? That sarcophagus is thousands of years old."

Tell me something I *don't know.* "Aren't they going to examine it today?" I looked pointedly at my watch. *Oh, damn.* The wine club party would be starting soon.

She huffed. "I'm leaving now." Pivoting on her low heels, she stormed away.

Leo stuck his dark head around the corner. "Was she talking about the sarcophagus?"

I sighed. "Yeah."

"Huh." He hesitated, watching Chelsea swish away. "Hey, I got those new tires on for you."

"Thanks. I appreciate it." I really did. Changing my tires was not part of Leo's job description. But he'd offered, and I'd happily accepted.

My assistant nodded and vanished around the corner.

At least it was unlikely Ronald had wrecked my tires. He'd been with me inside the library. But I would have preferred to tick him off my suspect list using brilliant deductions and incisive questioning instead of being a victim of vandalism.

Not that I was quite ready to put the building inspector in the clear for the murder. It was possible the tires had been random vandalism, that I'd just gotten unlucky.

My jaw tightened. I'd gotten the tires "gently used" online, and they'd *still* cost a bundle.

A broom handle clattered, and I hung my head. There's an old Polish saying: *Not my circus, not my monkeys.* Except this *was* my circus. For now though, the monkeys were going to have to carry on by their lonesomes.

I drove, windows down, to the winery. It was one of those California afternoons out of the movies—all golden warmth and sunshine. Grapevines glinted with the beginnings of autumn color, their leaves fluttering a greeting as my pickup bumped down the gravel drive to Plot 42.

Better and newer vehicles than mine had snagged all the shady spots beneath the weeping willow. I settled for leaving my windows down and throwing a towel over the wide steering wheel so I wouldn't get branded later.

Grapevines wound over the barn's dull-red wooden structure. Chrysanthemums bloomed beside the brick path. A chalkboard sign leaned beside the barn's closed door and proclaimed, *Yes, We're Open*, in cheerful orange script.

I opened the door and walked inside the coolness of the barn's tasting room. A wall of barrels stacked in metal racks by the open door hid a storage area. Upright barrels formed makeshift tables at random intervals on the cement floor.

The place was packed. People in jeans and neat blouses sipped wine at the tables and chatted in low voices. A long, polished wooden bar lined with customers ran along the right side of the room.

Extra groupings of chairs had been set up for today's tasting party. I scanned the barn.

Janice from Permitting stood around a wine barrel with another woman. Making my way to the bar, I nodded to Adele's father, pouring a glass for a silver-haired man. I realized with a start that Mr. Nakamoto's hair had begun to silver too. When had that happened?

He hurried down the bar toward me. "What can I get you, Maddie?"

"Got anything that pairs with existential angst?"

Without looking at the label, he poured a glass and handed it to me. "Malbec." He hurried away.

I took a sip, set it down, and smiled. *Mm*. Blackberry, plum, and... black cherry? I was feeling less angsty already.

And I didn't mind the liquid courage either. There was no reason for Janice to talk to me, and I steeled myself for some awkward conversation.

Shaking out my hands, I blew out a breath, grabbed my glass, and made my way to Janice's wine-barrel table. "Janice?" I asked with a delighted smile. "Is that you?"

The young woman glanced over her shoulder at me. Faint lines appeared between her brows. "Oh. Hi." She wore skinny jeans. Her mid-length brown hair just touched the shoulders of her white blouse.

"You probably don't remember my name. Maddie Kosloski. Paranormal Museum."

She laughed self-consciously. "I remembered. It's hard to forget your museum after..." She glanced down at the table's glass top.

"Ira," I said heavily. "Again, I'm so sorry for your loss."

She stiffened. "What's that supposed to mean?"

"Just... You worked together," I said uncertainly. Unless... Ira's ex had said he'd been having an affair with someone from work. She'd also said he'd liked them young. Could the girlfriend have been Janice?

"Awful thing," the other woman at the table said. She was a twenty-something redhead with a serious expression. "That poor man."

"Did you know him?" I asked.

"No," the redhead said. "But I heard about him. I'm Parker, by the way."

"Maddie," I said, and we shook hands. I smiled briefly. "But you probably already picked that up." I refocused on Janice. "Have the police said anything about who they think might have done it?"

"Why would they say anything to me?" Janice asked, squinting.

I grimaced. They wouldn't have. I'd just been making another hapless conversational foray. "I just thought... maybe it wasn't random. I thoguht the police might have said something about Ira being targeted."

"Why target Ira?" Janice asked.

"He *was* a player." Parker angled her head toward Janice, who flushed.

"What do you mean?" Ira's ex had said as much, but what did Janice's friend know?

"He was seeing Wynnona Cookson on the sly," Janice blurted.

I stared for a beat. "Cookson..." *The caterer's wife? Whoa.* That explained her reaction when Ira's body had been discovered. Had her husband known about the relationship?

"Ira broke it off with her," Janice continued. "She didn't take it well, I heard."

I cocked my head. "How did you hear all this?" Wynnona did *not* fit Ira's youngish dating profile. Could Janice be mistaken? Or intentionally trying to mislead?

"You hear things when you work with someone," Janice said.

"Town hall is a real hotbed of scandal," her friend drawled, and Janice shot her a dark look.

"You think Wynnona or her husband could have killed Ira?" I asked.

"How would I know who stuck his body in your sarcophagus?" Janice raised a brow. "It was *your* sarcophagus."

"Technically, we're a non-profit, so I don't exactly own..." *Not important.* I tried again. "Did Ira have any other enemies?"

"Anyone he gave a bad inspection report to." Janice's lip curled. "He inspected *your* museum."

"Well, he started to," I said. "We never got an inspection report from him." Because he'd been dead. I swallowed. "Did he get any threats at his office?"

"Not that I know of," Janice said.

"It just seems bizarre," I said. "I mean, killing a man is bad enough. Awful. Unthinkable. Unfortunately, it happens—too often. But staging the body in a sarcophagus like that—"

"It seems like a statement, doesn't it?" Parker tossed her hair. "Like something a serial killer would do."

A chill slithered down my spine. Serial killers featured prominently on the museum's wall of murderers. I really didn't want one in sleepy San Benedetto though. "Maybe the killer just needed to ditch the body. And there's only been one body." *So far.*

"But putting it in a sarcophagus?" Parker asked in a disbelieving tone. "At Ladies Aid? Only a total psycho would cross *those* women."

She had a point. "How has this affected your work?" I asked Janice.

The permitting specialist lifted one shoulder, dropped it. "Our work was affected when Ira disappeared. Not much has changed since then."

"Who's going to take Ira's place?" I asked.

Janice turned the goblet in her hand. "Ronald's bucking hard for the promotion. And he needs it."

"Oh?" I prompted, and Janice reddened.

Her friend braced an elbow on the wine barrel. "He's in debt. Big time. He'll do anything for the promotion, and I mean anything."

I stilled. Anything... *Including murder?*

chapter eleven

HAUNTED TIKI

1959, San Diego, CA

A *Tiki is a sculpture carved in the shape of a Polynesian god, spirit guardian, or spirit power. For Americans, Tikis became synonymous with the South Pacific during WWII. And when soldiers returned from the war, more South Pacific restaurants and bars opened in the US. Tiki culture took off.*

The museum's Tiki belonged to a popular surf bar in San Diego. The owner of the bar invented a tale about it being cursed to gin up business. But one night a drunken brawl broke out, and a man fell into the Tiki, hit his head, and died. The bar's clientele later became convinced the sculpture was haunted.

Playing amateur detective when you're dating a real detective is exactly the sort of thing to ruin a date night.

Except... it didn't. I told Jason what I'd learned (not much), he commiserated over the slashed tires, and then we had a perfectly lovely evening.

It was a little anticlimactic.

Not because we didn't fight. I'm old enough *not* to find those kinds of sparks interesting. Maybe we'd just reached the comfortable stage of our relationship? Maybe romance didn't matter?

And that was okay. Jason was a smart, honorable, kind man. And those things were more important than sparks.

So I didn't tell him my plans for tomorrow included attending Mark Spicer's cooperative gaming group. I didn't think Jason really wanted to know.

On the face of it, a cooperative gaming group seemed ideal for a chat. We'd all be cooperating while trying to beat the game. This meant talking.

What I hadn't realized was this meant talking about the game—not each other.

The three men stared at me expectantly. Gnawing my bottom lip, I studied the board, a gloomy building layout on a foreign planet. Tiny plastic aliens emerged from a gaping hole in the space-time continuum. It looked a lot like an orange that someone had jammed their thumb through.

We sat crammed around a plastic table in the corner of a room lined with rows of tables filled with gamers. A florescent light flickered, and I glanced up at the industrial ceiling.

I'd never noticed the place before—a game store with a coffee shop. It was a coffee shop with achingly slow service, but the draw was the gaming, not the cuisine. Aisles lined with games for sale jammed the far wall.

"So... I'm thinking I should use my range weapon?" I asked, doubtful.

"Can't," a bullet-shaped man named Tony rapped out. "You're too close."

How was I too close? "But my special power is the ability to use range weapons at close range, isn't it?"

Tony sighed. "Yes, but the rules don't say you can specifically use that power with this weapon."

"But they don't say I can't either," I argued. "Why would they give me a special power and then limit it like that?"

"If it's not in the rules," he said, "you can't do it."

Well, that was just dumb. Who operated like that? "But if I use my space grenade—"

"Interdimensional grenade," a redhead named Ken corrected, adjusting his glasses.

"Yeah," I said. "That. Won't I just blow up everyone in the room with me, like Mark?" I glanced at the building inspector. His florid face scrunched with concentration. Would I blow myself up too?

"It's okay." Mark swept a hand through his sandy hair. "I've got plenty of life points left. Do it."

Whatever. They understood the game better than I did. "Then I use my grenade." I picked up a die and rolled. The die clattered to a halt beside a plastic alien.

The building inspector winced. "Okay, I lose three life points."

"And you take out half the life points for all the aliens in the room," Tony said.

I slumped back in my chair. Only half? I hadn't *killed* any aliens? If I'd used my range weapon, I could have killed at least one of them. Now they'd all attack us at once.

Ken picked up a die.

"So what does everyone do here?" I asked. "For work, I mean."

"I teach math at San Benedetto Junior High," Tony said.

No wonder he was so bitter. "And you?" I asked Ken.

"I'm a plumber."

Okay that was... really cool. In California, guys in construction was hotter than CEOs. Plumbers were rarer *and* more useful. "Residential or commercial?"

"Commercial."

Even better. "I run the San Benedetto Paranormal Mus— History Museum. Can I have your card?"

Ken lifted one hip, pulled a wallet from the back pocket of his baggy jeans, and handed me a card.

"Thanks," I said.

Mark grunted. "You already know what I do."

"I don't know what you do," Tony said.

"Building inspector," Mark said.

Ken's eyes narrowed. He rolled the die. "Cool. I get an interdimensional grenade."

Relieved the die and all decisions were now out of my hands, I braced my elbows on the table. The plastic aliens wobbled. "So what do you do for fun? Aside from playing cooperative board games," I added.

"Play non-cooperative games," Tony said.

"Ah." I nodded. "The full gaming spectrum. And you?" I asked Mark.

Tony reached for the die. "I like to hunt."

In my plastic chair, I leaned a little away from him. "Really?" *With a gun?* Tony wasn't a suspect, but how *had* Ira died? He could have been shot for all I knew. Those cheesecloth bandages could have been covering all sorts of damage.

"What do you hunt?" I asked.

The teacher shrugged his thick shoulders. "Depends on the season. Ducks and wild boar, mostly."

"I hear wild boar is gamey," the plumber said.

"You need to know how to prepare it," Mark said.

"Do you hunt too?" I asked, and he nodded. "Do you, ah, butcher it yourself?" I asked. Maybe he'd stabbed Ira.

"No," he said. "I've got a guy."

"Where do you store the meat?" If he hunted, he might have a big enough freezer to store a body.

"My garage," he said. "Why?"

Ah ha! He *did* have an extra freezer. But I couldn't exactly ask if it was man-sized. "Just curious," I said. "With all the power outages we've been having, have you got a generator? I'm thinking of getting one for the museum." If I knew how big his generator was, maybe I could figure out the size of his freezer.

"Those are expensive," Tony said, reaching for the die.

Or maybe I was overcomplicating things. "If I can't keep the air conditioning running during the summer," I said. "I'll lose business." We'd been a balmy seventy-eight today, but summers could get brutal.

"You'll need a permit," Mark warned.

I forced a smile. Of course I would. In California, you weren't allowed to paint a wall without a permit. Not that that stopped anyone from doing it. "I'll apply. Do you need a very big freezer for your meat?"

"It's the size of a refrigerator," the building inspector said.

"What kind of generator do you have?" Tony asked.

"I don't," the building inspector said. "Last time the power went out, I had to run everything over to Ronald's. He's a prepper. You should see his set-up—gas *and* solar powered generators."

Whoa. Don't-call-me-Ronnie had a freezer big enough to store his stuff *and* Mark's? Ronald's freezer might actually be human-sized—ideal for storing Ira's body.

Tony laughed shortly and rolled. "Yeah, but you're set if the zombie apocalypse comes. You've got a boat. Dammit, I'm down to one life point." He added three more plastic aliens to the portal.

The others frowned. If one person died, everyone lost. Mark picked up the die.

"What kind of boat do you have?" I asked.

"Motor," the building inspector said, scanning the board.

"Uh," Ken said, "it's practically a yacht. We gamed on it in the summer," he said to me.

Mark rolled and cursed. "I'm dead."

The others groaned. Tony glared at me.

"You said you had enough life points for me to blow you up," I said, defensive.

"I didn't realize you were going to blow me up that badly," Mark said.

I folded my arms. "I didn't know what I was going to roll."

Tony picked up the plastic aliens and put them in the box. "That's it for me. I've gotta stop at the store before I get home."

Grumbling, the others gathered up the cards. I sorted mine into neat piles. "I'm thinking of getting an extra freezer," I said to Mark. "Do you have an upright or a, er, lying down freezer?"

"A chest freezer," he said.

That would be more convenient for body storage. "Like Ronald's?"

He gave me an odd look. "Yeah."

I lingered as we cleaned up the game, hoping to have more time to chat. But Ken lingered too. The three of us walked out into the mini-mall parking lot together.

I wandered to my pickup and watched Mark get into a Tesla. The sight of the expensive car just made me grumpier. Yes, they were probably the best made cars in America today. But there were just so *many* of them in California.

They were also expensive. A fancy car? A nice boat? How much did building inspectors earn?

And more importantly, did Janice have a freezer big enough for a body too? I started my pickup. It was something I was going to have to find out.

chapter twelve

HAUNTED MOLINILLO—RATTLES WHEN A Lie Is Told.

Mexico, circa 1900

This wooden whisk is traditionally used to mix Mexican hot cocoa.

"They're *still* not giving the sarcophagus back." Chelsea's eyes blazed. She folded her arms over her little black dress. "Can you believe it? They found absolutely nothing inside the sarcophagus aside from sarcophagus, and they won't give it back."

Well, that was disappointing. Was absence of evidence, evidence? "They didn't damage it, did they?" I leaned forward, resting my elbows on my desk. One nice thing about the new paranormal museum was I had an actual office. With a door.

The high windows provided natural lighting. Artifacts from the old museum lined the shelves on the walls. A molinillo. A spirit board. A faded pair of ballet shoes.

The new museum had enough artifacts to rotate and put on actual themed shows. The artifacts in my office would eventually get back out onto the floor. But for now, I got to enjoy them in relative solitude.

"No." Chelsea huffed a breath. She paced in front of a bookcase lined with tomes on museum management and fundraising. "But we can't control what happens to the sarcophagus while it's in the evidence lockup. I told them how to care for it, but they admitted they couldn't guarantee anything. The *police* will have it."

"And I've spoken to Detective Slate about that." I rolled a pencil between my fingers. "He knows they need to be careful with the sarcophagus."

"I mean, it's obvious they won't find the murder weapon inside the sarcophagus at this point. Why keep it?"

"Obvious?"

"The victim was bludgeoned with a wide, curving object." She made an open circle with her hands about six inches wide.

I blinked. "They told you that?"

"No, I overheard the crime scene techs talking. Apparently the coroner had to wait for the body to completely defrost before determining cause of death. But even frozen they could see the dent in his head."

I grimaced. I hadn't seen beneath Ira's bandages, and for that I was glad. Uncovering clues—even via Chelsea—was all well and good. But hearing the gruesome details was a more palatable experience than seeing them first hand.

"What else did they say about the body?" I asked.

"Nothing. The museum hasn't even opened, and everything's cursed."

"This *is* a paranormal museum." And as much as I hated to admit it, our soft opening wasn't all bad news. The body in the sarcophagus had gotten us a disturbing amount of press. The story had even been picked up internationally.

"And your new *assistant* is mounting the title cards crookedly."

I sighed and hung my head. I'd thought giving Jordan something more interesting to do than sweeping might improve his work ethic. So far, it hadn't.

"I'll talk to him," I said. "And since we can't control what the police do, maybe we should focus on what we can control."

Her expression pinched. "You mean what *I* can control."

And why did *that* sound accusatory? The phone rang on the desk. Automatically, I picked it up. "San Benedetto Paranormal Mus— History Museum, this is Maddie speaking."

Chelsea's delicate nostrils flared. Her jaw jutted forward. She strode from my office, leaving the door open behind her.

"This is Peter Sears from the San Francisco Daily News," a man said. "I'd like to talk to you about the body in your sarcophagus."

I tipped back my head, forced my neck muscles to unclench, and studied the speckled tile ceiling. This wasn't the first reporter to call. Since I couldn't discuss the body, I'd decided five reporters ago to focus on the history of the sarcophagus.

I expounded for a good five minutes on sarcophagi, ancient Egyptian myth and magic, and the museum itself before the reporter interrupted me.

"And the body?" he asked.

"No idea. That's a better question for the police."

"I understand Ira Myatt inspected your new museum."

Oh, crud. He'd figured that out? The other reporters hadn't. "Yes," I admitted, dread spiraling in my gut. "I did meet him briefly."

"Did he indicate whether the museum had failed the inspection?"

"No. It was only our first inspection. He pointed out some minor issues, and we addressed them. That was the last I saw of Ira."

"Because he was dead."

"I don't know about that." I shifted in my executive chair. "When *was* he killed?" Chelsea had done a better job than I at sniffing out clues. Maybe the reporter had a few to give.

"No idea. But he *was* killed. And he was found in one of the museum's exhibits... *after* inspecting your museum."

My fingertips hurt, and I glanced down. I was crushing them into my chair's faux leather. Drawing a long breath, I unclenched my hand. "Obviously, someone put him there later. That sarcophagus was empty when we moved it into Ladies Aid."

"Who could have done that?"

"No idea." And I shouldn't have even said that much. "Sorry, I need to go. Good luck with your article." I hung up and flopped back in my chair.

I gnawed my bottom lip. No one could seriously think anyone at the museum would hide a body in one of our own sarcophagi. Could they?

Of course they could. But I couldn't control what people thought. So taking my own advice, I focused on what I could control and went to find Jordan in our special collection room.

The special collection space took pride of place in the center of the labyrinth. A big, wide, square room for our rotating exhibits, it was what I hoped would draw repeat business to the museum.

The exhibit we'd planned for our grand opening was *Alchemy*. Part of our new collection included alchemical texts that were centuries old. Herb had displayed alembics and other accoutrements of the alchemist's art. We'd included an online presentation describing the impact of alchemy on modern psychology, science, and occult thought.

Jordan stared at an empty pedestal. He looked at the title card in his hand and at the pedestal again. Light from the mismatched chandeliers glinted off his shaggy blond hair.

"Problem?" I asked lightly, and the pre-teen jumped. "Sorry," I said. "I didn't mean to startle you."

He scowled. "You didn't."

Okay then. "How's it going?" I looked around the walls. Chelsea was right. The title cards were all askew.

He shrugged. "Okay, I guess."

I walked to a particularly crooked card beside a painting of an alchemist. "This one's a little crooked. Is the level I gave you working?" *Or are you just not using it?*

He shrugged again. "I guess."

I bit back my irritation. In fairness, I hadn't exactly been cheery sweetness and light at Jordan's age either. And the point wasn't the quality of his work. The point was that he was working, paying off his debt to society. Or at least to the museum.

"Let me see." I picked the laser level off the floor, aligned it on the wall beneath the painting, and pressed the button. A red laser beam cut across the top corner of the card. "It looks like this one's a little off." Carefully, I peeled the title card free of the wall and realigned it. "There. See? If the bubble lands between the two lines, it's straight." I pointed.

He rolled his eyes. "I know. My dad showed me how."

My heart squeezed. I was having trouble managing Jordan for a few hours. How was Mason dealing with being a single parent full-time? It had all been sprung on him so quickly—first learning of his son, then his fiancée taking off...

"Okay," I said. "I'll leave you to it. Would you please double check the other title cards and make sure they're straight too?"

I hurried from the room and nearly flattened my mother studying a display of spirit boards. I bit back a yelp. "What are you doing here?" I asked.

My mother patted her pixie-cut hair. "I came to take you to lunch, of course." She was dressed in a long, cream colored coat and matching turtleneck.

"Of course?" My eyes narrowed. She hadn't mentioned anything about lunch. My mother was up to something.

"It's Monday," she said blandly.

I eyed her with suspicion. "Are we doing Monday lunches now?"

She tucked her arm in mind and drew me back down the charcoal corridor. "Why not? Oh, have I caught you at a bad time? You look frazzled."

"No, I'm not—" Hold on. I brightened. My mother knew about kids. She'd managed me and my siblings, and we'd been handfuls. "Jordan's working today."

"Ah, yes. His community service at the museum."

My gaze flicked upward. Of course she knew about that too. Why wouldn't she?

"How's that going?" she continued.

"He's a little, ah—"

"Sullen?"

"Something like that."

"It's to be expected," she said. "None of you were much fun to be around at that age either."

Fair. "So how'd you deal with us?" I asked. We climbed the steps to the lobby.

"Boundaries, accountability, and discipline," she said.

I nodded. "Uh, huh."

Herb stuck his head around the corner. His eyes widened behind his thick glasses, and he ducked away.

My mouth puckered. I hadn't spoken to Herb since he'd requested approval for his course. And come to think of it, that was weird. Usually he'd be checking up on his request's status at least once a day. "Herb—"

"I know you feel guilty about what happened to Jordan's mother." She squeezed my arm. "But you did nothing wrong."

I slowed. I hadn't told my mother I felt guilty. Was it that obvious?

"And if you want to build a healthy connection with him," she said, "you need to play your proper role, as his boss. You're not his friend, so don't try to be one. You're an adult. He's a child." She stopped beside the ticket counter. The golden glow from the circus-style lights glinted off the silver threads in her hair. My mother smiled. "You're doing the right thing, letting him work here. It will help him feel like part of the community." She cocked her head. "What's wrong?"

"Nothing," I said. "Just thinking about what you said about connection. When I was overseas, I never felt like I was part of a community. I had friends, of course, but not the kind of connection I have here with you, my friends, with Jason."

But an uncomfortable sensation twinged in my chest—the feeling of a lie. But what had I said that wasn't true?

"Yes," she said, "those things are important. We don't realize how much until we lose them. Or find them."

Jason. Absently, I rubbed my chest. What was wrong with my connection to him? Wasn't it as strong as it should be? But we were good. In a groove. I was being ridiculous.

I shook myself. "Where are we going for lunch?"

"I thought we'd go downtown," she said vaguely, moving toward the exit.

I stopped short and stuffed my hands in the pockets of my hoodie. "Where downtown?"

She tapped her chin. "Oh, I don't know... What about Ladies Aid?"

"Ladies...?" *Augh.* I should have known. "No. No way. You don't want to take me to lunch. You want me to make a report to your cabal."

She laughed lightly. "Cabal? Oh, Maddie. You've always had such a delightful imagination. I understand the museum is sponsoring the Harvest Festival? Are you going?"

"No, no, no. You can't distract me with festival talk. I'm being shanghaied."

My mother tugged me toward the glass doors. "Nonsense. When have you turned down lunch and conversation?"

My belly knotted. *Lunch and conversation?* It all sounded so innocuous. Innocent, even. But if I knew Ladies Aid—and I did—I needed to prepare myself for *injurious* and *incriminating.*

chapter thirteen

Magic Scroll

Gondar, Ethiopia, circa 1880

These protective amulets were used to ward off illness and bad luck. Personalized and cut to be the exact height of the owner, scrolls would be worn in a case around the owner's neck.

The scrolls display influences from Muslim, Christian, and Jewish sources and are written in Ge'ez, the liturgical language of the Ethiopian Coptic Church. This scroll is made of goat vellum and is opened to an image of a demon trap. The scroll were believed to trap demons or evil spirits in the vicinity, rendering them powerless to harm the wearer or anyone else.

Community institutions like Ladies Aid are the true backbone of our society. Forget the federal government—it's more likely to screw things up and triple the price tag. State government is little better—at least in a state the size of California.

Local government is more responsive, but it's still beholden to the feds and the state for money. If you want to improve your community, it's the local organizations that make the real difference.

At least that's what I kept telling myself.

"Fill this with water, will you?" My mom handed me a massive electric kettle and nodded toward the linoleum counter.

I lugged it to the oversized metal sink. "So what's the occasion?"

"Oh, no occasion." My mother dumped a bag of chocolate chips into a double boiler on the electric stove.

"Really." Disbelieving, I glanced at a silver tray of neatly aligned strawberries. "Chocolate covered strawberries are just *what you do*?"

"At Ladies Aid, we believe in making an occasion of things."

My mouth pursed. I turned to the sink and filled the kettle with water. "Occasion of what?"

"Oh, you know. Just the day."

"And my status report?" I guessed.

"The members *are* eager to hear what you've learned about the murder."

I *knew* it. I knew there was an ulterior motive. "I'm not doing it." I set the heavy kettle on the counter. "I'm not a member, and I'm not reporting. I've got nothing to report."

My mother laughed. "Don't be silly. Of course you do. We know you've been asking questions about the murder."

"How do you know that?"

Stirring the chocolate, she turned from the stove and cocked her head. "Seriously? Do you have any idea how many of our members have relatives working at Town Hall?"

I sighed. Actually, I did have a pretty good idea.

She pointed toward a white-painted cupboard. "Get the electric fondue pot, will you? It's on the top shelf."

Standing on tiptoe, I slid the pot from its shelf. The silvery lid slid off, and I caught it before it hit the linoleum floor. "Why would anyone at Town Hall assume I was interrogating Ira's coworkers?"

"There was no assumption about it. The inspectors have been comparing notes. You weren't very subtle at that astrophotography group."

No, I hadn't been. *Uranus.* Heh, heh.

I peered into the fondue pot. It looked clean, but I wiped it with a damp paper towel anyway. "If it gets back to Laurel—"

"I'm quite sure it already has."

"—that I'm reporting to Ladies Aid like an unlicensed private investigator—"

"Really, Madelyn, it's only fair. The body was found in *your* sarcophagus."

"The museum's."

"It wouldn't have been here if Ladies Aid hadn't thrown their support behind the museum expansion."

I squinted. "And making a report to Ladies Aid will help you politically."

"That too. People feel better when they know action is being taken."

Even if the action wasn't particularly helpful. But she was right. Sometimes doing nothing was the better play, but it satisfied no one.

"I've been researching Italian wedding toasts," my mother said.

I groaned. *My sister's wedding again?*

"Do not roll your eyes at me, young lady," she said severely. "This is an important moment in Melanie's life."

"I know, I know."

"One traditional toast is *Per Cent'anni*," she said in a decent imitation of an Italian accent. "It means *for a hundred years*. Isn't that romantic?"

"Yes," I said flatly.

She laughed. "Wait until you and Jason are in Sicily together. You'll think it's romantic then."

Jason and me on a romantic Italian island... Maybe that would up the romance quotient in our relationship? Maybe a Sicilian vacation was what we needed.

My mother's co-president, Cora, wafted into the kitchen. Her pale blue caftan rippled around her curvaceous form. Silver, moon goddess earrings dangled from her ears.

Cora removed a plastic-wrapped tray of sandwiches from the refrigerator. "Everything on track?"

My mother nodded. "Everything."

And somehow, I knew they weren't just talking about the food prep. But since none of this had exactly been a surprise, I was finding it hard to muster up much righteous indignation. Ladies Aid was gonna Ladies Aid.

We finished prepping the food and moved it into the Grand Hall. I piled my plate. I'd probably just end up with food stuck in my teeth when I made my report, but I was determined to at least get a full belly out of the coming debacle.

After a time, the ladies assembled, chattering in rows of metal folding chairs. On the dais, my mother moved behind the podium. She tapped the microphone, and the ladies fell silent.

"Thank you for coming, everyone," my mother said. "I know we've all been concerned about the status of the investigation."

In the front row, hatchet-faced Eliza snorted.

"Madelyn has kindly agreed to come here to give you an update," my mother continued, unperturbed. She nodded to me. "Madelyn?"

My stomach butterflied. I swallowed and climbed the steps to the podium. "Uh, hi, everyone."

The microphone screeched. My audience winced.

I cleared my throat. "As many of you know, I've had the opportunity to *chat* with Ira's closest colleagues." *Not interrogate, not investigate.* "Ira was a bit of a loner, aside from, er... His wife mentioned he'd had an affair with one of the women in the office."

A wave of murmurs rippled through the hall.

"I don't know who," I said.

"Of course not," Eliza said dryly.

"There are a lot of women in Town Hall," I sputtered and glanced at my mother. "I don't suppose any of you have heard any rumors?"

The women looked at each other. No one responded.

My shoulders hunched. Well, Ladies Aid wasn't infallible. "An affair could point to motive."

"Not if the woman in question is single," Eliza pointed out.

"The only other enemies Ira may have had were her his co-workers who wanted his job, and business owners who he didn't pass on inspection," I said.

"Like you?" Eliza asked.

"Madelyn would hardly bring a body to her own museum's soft opening," my mother said tartly.

"Of course not," Cora said, her tone soothing. "But that does bring up the question of who would, and why?"

"Obviously, to get rid of the body in a way that moved the attention away from the killer." Eliza's voice dripped with derision.

"So." I coughed. "The obvious question remains. Where was Ira between the time he disappeared and when he reappeared in the sarcophagus—?"

"No," Eliza said, "the obvious question is who killed him."

"And it appears he was in a freezer prior to appearing in the sarcophagus," I said.

"That much was already clear." Eliza folded her arms. The other women muttered.

"Which is actually a useful, er, clue." My hands curled in my hoodie's pockets. *Clues. Who was I? Nancy Drew?* "Most people don't have access to a freezer large enough to store a body in."

"What about your donor, that cryonics person?" Eliza asked. "*He* could have easily stored a body."

I bit the inside of my lip. Frank's company *had* been inspected by Ira. "It's a possibility."

"Have you talked to him?" Eliza demanded.

"Not yet," I admitted. How was I supposed to have time for interrogations when I was trying to start up a museum?

"It does seem a rather obvious oversight," my mother said.

My gaze flicked toward the high ceiling. *Thanks, Mom.*

"I hope you're not hanging your entire investigation on the body being frozen." Eliza motioned toward the door to the kitchen. "We have a walk-in freezer."

"Surely you're not suggesting one of our members was responsible?" my mother asked coolly.

Eliza colored. "That's not—"

An alarm blared.

"Fire!" Eliza shouted. "Everyone out."

I sniffed, my heart jumping. The acrid scent of smoke filled the room, but the air looked clear.

My mother leapt to her feet, the metal chair clattering to its side. "The kitchen." She pointed.

My chest squeezed. Curls of black smoke seeped from beneath the door.

chapter fourteen

PLANCHETTE

UK, 1866

This example of a planchette/spirit writing device may have a pencil inserted in the hole in its top for spirit writing. It can also be used on a spirit or Ouija board. This particular example, manufactured by Kirby and Company in the 1860s, was called the Physio-Psychophone. However, the idea of a planchette for spirit writing originated during a séance in France in 1853. The spirits suggested taking a basket, turning it upside down, jamming a pencil into it, and séance participants putting their hands on the basket so the spirits could write messages.

In later years, planchettes developed more of a heart shape. Another 20th century innovation added round windows in the top of the planchette. This enabled easier viewing of the letters on the board beneath. You can find all these, as well as a more modern planchette/board combo, in the displays adjacent.

"All right, ladies. You know the drill." Cora strode to the exit and opened the door. A breath of cool, autumn air flowed into the Grand Hall. The women formed a line and began leaving the hall.

I went to the back of the line, then realized my mother wasn't in it. My teeth ground. The kitchen door, billowing black smoke, swung slowly shut.

Cursing, I raced to the kitchen and yanked the door open. It was just like my mother to try to take care of a fire herself, so I shouldn't be angry.

She was taking charge, assessing the situation. It was what made her great. It also might get her killed.

My legs trembled. "Mom?" I pressed my sleeve to my nose and coughed, my eyes burning. The kitchen was a charcoal smear of blurred shapes. "Mom!" I froze, gulping back a breath, unsure where to move.

Whoosh.

"There's a second fire extinguisher by the door," she shouted.

I gasped, relief loosening my muscles, and sucked in a lungful of smoke. Coughing, I fumbled, and my hands touched cool metal. "Where are you?"

"At the stove." There was another whooshing sound. "Open the window. I can't see a thing."

I wasn't sure adding more oxygen to the situation was going to improve things. The door was closer. I used its kickdown stopper to prop it open. More smoke filtered out. I could make out my mother's slim form beside the stove.

She coughed. Metal clanged to the floor. "Where's that extinguisher?"

I hurried to the stove and handed her the extinguisher. She sprayed the stove and wall behind it. "Window!"

I stumbled to a window and grasped its frame, yanking upward. It stuck.

Blood pounded in my head. I gave a second heave. It didn't move. Swearing, I hurried to the next window. It slid up easily. Fresh air flowed into the kitchen, and more smoke cleared.

My mother swept her hand over the stove, and objects clattered to the floor. A squat, half-melted can rolled against my foot, and I kicked it away.

She angled her body and sprayed behind the appliance. "That'll do it," she rasped.

I bent, hands on my knees. "You sure?" I asked, worried. My mother was no fragile elder. She wouldn't want me making a big deal over this. But though I was grudgingly impressed by her successful swift action, she was still my mother.

In the distance, a siren wailed.

She set the empty red canister on the counter and leaned against it. "I'm sure I turned off the stove when I was finished," she fretted.

"Let's get out of here," I said and moved toward the door, hoping she'd follow.

To my relief, she did. My mother and I joined the ladies in the parking lot.

"You shouldn't have followed me," she said sharply.

"And you shouldn't have played fireman." My voice rose.

"I had to see if I could put it out. Which I did."

Cora wafted toward us, her kaftan fluttering. "Are you two all right?"

My mother coughed and nodded, one fisted hand to her mouth. "The fire's out."

"The kitchen?" Cora asked.

"The stove," my mother said.

Eliza emerged from behind Cora. "Weren't *you* using the stove, Fran?"

My mother straightened. It was hard to tell beneath the soot on her face, but she seemed to redden. "Yes. I was."

A fire truck turned into the parking lot, followed by an ambulance. A blue muscle car sped behind them, and my stomach tightened.

"You were in fact," Eliza continued loudly, "the *only* person to use the stove."

My jaw clenched. Leave it to Eliza to use this as an opportunity for a political hit job. "I might have used it too," I said.

My mother shot me a look. "You did not. There's no need to protect me. I turned that stove off. There must be something defective about it."

"And who's fault is that if it was?" Eliza said. "As co-presidents, you and Cora are in charge of maintaining the equipment."

My mother's mouth compressed.

"I should talk to the fire department." Cora hurried toward the fire truck.

"Help," a weak voice called from behind us. "Maribel's having a heart attack."

"Administer CPR!" My mother jogged toward the firemen. Eliza huffed. She strode toward a small cluster of women, presumably gathered around the luckless Maribel.

A shadow loomed over me. I shivered.

"Kosloski," Laurel snarled. "What did you do?"

My shoulders hunched, my mouth going dry. "Nothing," I rasped. "There was a kitchen fire."

A group of firemen trotted into the Ladies Aid Grand Hall. Two jogged toward the circle of women.

"And were you *in* the kitchen?" Laurel asked me.

I rubbed my throat. "Well, do you mean after the fire started or before?"

"Both."

I folded my arms, and an acrid odor billowed from my museum hoodie. "Yes."

Laurel's nose wrinkled. "Yes to which?"

"To both."

"So you left something on the stove, and a fire started."

"I did not." Mulishly, I stuck my jaw forward. "And aren't you getting a little bored blaming me for everything that goes wrong?"

"But you make it so easy."

My nostrils flared, weight building behind my forehead. Seriously? She was doing this now? "That's—" *Oh.* I *was* making it easy by responding, reacting. I needed to do better. And I started by walking away. Laurel didn't bother to call after me.

Maribel was taken to the hospital. The firemen declared the fire officially out and agreed something had been left on the stove. Unofficially, the ladies agreed it was a good thing they hadn't barricaded the Great Hall's door, since the lock was still broken.

I puzzled over that. But if someone had snuck in to start the fire, they hadn't used the broken door to the Grand Hall. It had been filled with women.

Which meant the fire probably had just been a dumb accident. And my mother wasn't prone to dumb accidents.

I glanced at the building. The door to the Grand Hall stood open. My mother emerged, looked around, and closed it.

I studied the pavement. Could someone have gotten into the lodge another way? Or was I grasping at straws, trying to let my mother off the hook?

I needed to start eating healthier if I was going to fit into my bridesmaid dress, So instead of ordering a pizza, I drove to the grocery store for Greek yogurt, fruit, and granola.

In the produce department, the caterer's wife, Wynnona frowned at a basket of strawberries. She put it into her green basket.

The nice thing about small-town amateur detecting is suspects and witnesses tend to be within easy reach. I wasn't about to pass up this advantage. "Hi," I said, striding toward her and jamming up my sleeves. "Wynnona, right?"

She blinked at me. "Yes?"

"I'm Maddie, from the paranormal museum. Your husband catered the soft opening?"

"Oh, right. Sorry." She clawed a hand through her curling brown hair. "That night was... Well, you know."

"Yeah," I said, rueful. "Me and the museum were the least memorable part of that night. Alex's food was great, though."

Wynnona smiled. "He really is an amazing chef." She glanced into her basket. A bottle of champagne angled in its corner. "It makes cooking something for him a little stressful though. How can I compare? But I think I should be safe with steak."

"Steak, champagne and strawberries? Sounds like a romantic evening."

An odd expression crossed her face. "I'm trying. Well, have a good evening." She walked away.

I stared after her, trying to define what I'd seen in her eyes. It hadn't been the soft glow of anticipated romance. Had it been guilt? Shaking my head, I collected my things, paid, and went home to a lonely but healthy meal.

I thought of calling Jason, but he was working. Maybe the reason I'd been feeling so disconnected from him was me. Maybe I should do something romantic for him. Maybe cook him dinner.

I came up with promotions for a paranormal museum on a weekly basis. I should be able to come up with *something* fun for the two of us to do. I drummed my fingers on the kitchen table.

An activity? Shared activities were supposed to bring people closer. We'd be going to the upcoming Harvest Festival together, so that was something. But it also felt a little lazy. Maybe we could go to Tahoe. It would be less crowded this time of year. His birthday was coming up. I could surprise him with a trip.

I set my bowl in the sink, went to the dining room, and opened my laptop on the blue couch. There were all sorts of cabins available. The lakeview ones were the most expensive, but what the heck? Why not make an occasion of it? Excited, I made a list of possible cabins and went to bed imagining winter hikes and crackling fires.

The next morning my throat still felt raw. I hauled myself to the new museum to feed GD. "I'm here," I shouted from my office.

The cat didn't respond. Since this was not unusual, I shrugged it off. I scooped a cup of kibble from the bin and let it rattle into the bowl. The black cat eeled around the door and into the room.

"I thought that would get your attention," I said dryly.

Ignoring me, the cat stuck his head in the bowl and crunched kibble.

I refilled the water bowl, settled in behind my industrial metal desk, and called the caterer.

"Cookson catering," he answered. "This is Alex. How can I help you?"

"Hi, it's Maddie from the museum."

"Oh, hi. Has the date for the opening been finalized?"

"Yes," I lied, and my stomach quivered. But I *was* going to have my grand opening as planned, come hell, high water, or invidious inspectors. "What do you need from me?"

"The down payment. Unless there are any changes to the menu?"

"No," I said. "No changes. Hey, did you hear about the fire in the Ladies Aid kitchen yesterday?"

"No. Was anyone hurt?"

"One of the women had a minor heart attack, but she's recovering. It looks like she'll be okay."

"That's awful," he said. "I mean, it's good that she's recovering. But a heart attack... I've heard heart attacks really hurt. A lot."

I leaned back in my executive chair and stared out the open door and past the ticket booth. "We're trying to figure out what may have caused it. When you were in the kitchen last week, did you notice any hazards?"

"Quite a few. But that's not unusual in kitchens like that. It's why I prefer to do most of my meal prep back in my shop."

I perked up in my chair. "Ah, specifically?"

"The fan over the stove wasn't working. Flammable materials were on the counters too close to the stove. I shifted them, of course, but who's to say someone didn't move them back? Um... And I believe the wire in one of the electric kettles was frayed. I pointed it all out to one of the women in charge—I believe her name was Eliza?"

I stiffened. *Eliza.* She'd known about all the hazards. But would she have started the fire just to make my mother and Cora look bad?

chapter fifteen

BENEDETTO GOBLET

Spain, circa 17th century

This "siphon glass" was brought to California by Salvador Morales, one of the first landowners in what would become San Benedetto. The glass was cursed after Morales's murder.

The blue straw in the glass is the remains of the "surprise" siphon gag. It caused a stream of liquid to escape through a hole in the side of the glass, dampening the victim of the prank.

The only thing more irritating than being wrong is when someone you dislike is right. A cryonics facility was ideal for storing unwanted bodies. It was their whole reason for existence. I just wish Eliza hadn't pointed that out.

I walked into Frostova's spa-like reception area, my sneakers silent on the wooden floor. The high-ceilinged room's marbleized turquoise walls were likely meant to symbolize all things cold. But they just looked modern and glam.

Though I had an appointment, my stomach fluttered. If Frank Frost was involved in the inspector's murder, I didn't care if I offended him. If he wasn't, I didn't want to lose a museum sponsor. And I wasn't sure if I could ask him what I needed and thread that needle.

A twenty-something receptionist in a white lab coat, her hair in a high bun, smiled. "Welcome to Frostova. How can I help you?" A sleek turquoise sign hung on the wall behind her.

"I'm Maddie Kosloski. I've got an appointment with Frank for 10:30."

She studied her screen. Her manicured fingers tapped the keyboard. "Ah, yes. Let me call him and let him know you're here."

"Thanks."

I ambled to a curving chair and sat. It was the most comfortable chair I've ever planted myself in, and I let my head drop back. The ceiling was white and textured with wavy lines, like a field of snow after a heavy wind.

"Maddie?" a man asked.

I jerked, blinking in the lounge chair. My chest heated. Had I fallen asleep?

"Sorry if I woke you." Frank grinned down at me and brushed back his near-white hair.

I forced myself upright. "No, it's... This is a really comfortable chair." I lurched from it awkwardly and shot an embarrassed glance at the receptionist.

"It's from Iceland," my donor said, as if that explained everything. "Let's go to my office."

I followed him up an elevator to the third floor and down a hallway to a wide room. A middle-aged brunette in a fitted lab coat looked up from the desk and smiled.

"Maddie, this is Tessa. She keeps things running around here."

Tessa smiled. "Which is a fancy way to call me his executive assistant. It's nice to meet you."

"Hi." We shook hands.

"Come in." Frank opened a door to another office.

I walked past him and inside. One wall in the office was of that marbleized turquoise. The rest were snow white. Picture windows overlooked the parking lot.

Frank strolled around a modern, blond-wood desk. He sat in a white leather executive chair. The CEO motioned me toward the two smaller, matching chairs opposite.

I sat, and the leather made an embarrassing squeak beneath my jeans. I coughed. "I don't know if you've been following the press, but the soft opening got more attention than we expected."

One corner of his mouth lifted. "I *did* notice. It's the first time I've felt terrible about publicity."

"Yes, your sign was in most of the photos from the, er, event." It had been right behind the Egyptian exhibit where the body had been found. "I put together a list of all the media that included a photo of your sign or mention of your company." I slid a USB drive across the desk to him.

"I suppose the real Grand Opening will be even better attended by the press," he said. "I know we'd already planned a dollar amount to sponsor that, but I'm willing to up it by five thousand."

I gulped down my avarice. *An extra five grand for the opening...* I wasn't even sure how I could spend the money. *Stop counting your chickens. He's a suspect.* "Maybe we can get a Halloween-themed ice sculpture?"

He laughed. "Brilliant."

It seemed a little on-the-nose to me. I looked down at the wood floor. *And enough procrastinating.* "I heard you knew the man who died?"

He sobered. "That building inspector. I wouldn't say I knew him, but I'd encountered him."

"I can't imagine what sort of building codes apply to a facility like yours." *Or how to direct this conversation.*

His blue eyes rolled. "Neither could the inspectors. I had to explain most of the codes to them."

"That must have been a little frustrating," I said.

"You have no idea."

"Were they decent about it?"

He raised a pale brow. "Decent?"

I'd gone too far, but I blundered onward. "Willing to work with you on things."

He stiffened in his white leather chair. "I don't know what you mean."

"There was some confusion about the ADA rules for an old building like mine," I said quickly. "It turns out I hadn't filed the proper paperwork for those rules to apply. Fortunately, they let me file the paperwork and backdate it."

His shoulders dropped. He sank back in his chair. "Ah. Well, this was a completely new facility. Would you like to see more of it?"

I relaxed. I *hadn't* gone too far—or at least I'd covered for it. *But his reaction...* I glanced sidelong at the wooden door. "A tour? Sure."

He rose and led me to the door. "How would you like to try cryotherapy? It would make you a better ambassador if you've experienced it yourself."

"Ah... Does it involve getting cold?"

"That *is* the point," he said dryly. "But it's only for two minutes." He strode down the ice-blue hallway, and I followed. "First you'll go into a chamber at minus seventy-six degrees Fahrenheit—"

"Naked?" I yelped.

"No, no. You'll wear protective earmuffs and gloves and shoes, as well as shorts and a tank top. After thirty seconds in that chamber, you'll step into the second chamber, which is at minus one hundred and sixty-six degrees Fahrenheit. All you do is ninety seconds there, and you're out. It feels amazing."

If I survived. "Yeah, I can imagine surviving an Arctic near-death experience would."

"The aim is to drop your body temperature by fifty degrees."

"Why?" I asked, incredulous. Who would put themselves through that?

"Aside from being incredibly relaxing, it reduces migraines, arthritic pain, treats skin conditions... There are a host of benefits we're still discovering. Want to try it?"

Two minutes of cold? I had a feeling it would be a long two minutes. But he *was* a sponsor, and one I'd just narrowly avoided insulting. "Ah. Yeah. Sure. Why not?" I rubbed the back of my neck. "And the cryonics process?"

"You don't want to try that until after you're dead." He laughed shortly. "Or at least *legally* dead."

I don't trust hairsplitting. It's usually a cover for something illegal or immoral. I cleared my throat. "Legally dead? What do you mean?"

"Legally dead is when the heart stops. Totally dead is when the brain stops. If there's to be any chance of reviving the body after it's frozen, the body has to go in while there's still some cellular function in the brain."

Okay, that actually made sense, and I shoved my suspicions aside. "Got it."

"The entry to the cryotherapy is separate from that to our offices and the cryonics facilities. We don't want people getting confused."

We stopped in front of a smaller reception desk. The windowed room overlooked a separate parking lot. A forty-something blond behind the desk smiled. "Hello, Mr. Frost."

"Hi, Marla. This is Maddie. She'd like to try our cryotherapy chambers."

"Of course." She flipped through an appointment book and nodded. "Right this way." She took me into a locker room and handed me a bundle of black clothing. "Change into these, then we'll take your temperature."

"Okay," I said uncertainly.

I waited for her to leave, then I changed into the tank and volley-ball-style shorts. I looked at myself in the mirror. In the black mittens, booties, and earmuffs, I looked like a dyspeptic penguin.

I stuck my head into the reception area. Frank had vanished. Uneasy, I looked around the sleek blue and white room.

Marla smiled. "All set?"

I edged farther into the room. "I guess."

"Let's take your temperature." She zapped my forehead with an electronic thermometer. "Ninety-four point two degrees. You run cool."

I wasn't feeling very cool. My heart jittered, which was silly. But lots of people did this. Getting me into a cryotherapy chamber wasn't part of a dastardly plot to murder me. Not with Marla as a witness.

She led me back through the locker room to what looked like a glassed-in shower. "Okay, the important thing to know is you're in control. If it gets too cold for you, all you need to do is step out." Her upper lip curled.

I have a big imagination, but I didn't need it to pick up on the subtext. Only filthy cowards ejected prematurely.

Uncertainly, I smiled. "Got it."

"In you go." She handed me a black face mask. "You don't want your lips to freeze."

I hooked it over my ears. She opened the door to the first chamber. "Try not to tense your muscles," she said.

I stepped inside the white-walled room, the pad on the floor soft beneath me. The air was sharp as a blade. *Everything* tensed. At least the face mask smothered my craven yelp.

The door snicked shut behind me. Panicked, I turned to face the glass. Marla gave me a thumbs up. "You can do it," she said, her voice muffled by the glass.

Don't tense my muscles? How the hell was I supposed to manage that? I counted the seconds, my teeth chattering. *One-Mississippi, relax, two-Mississippi, relax...* I hated this. Why had I agreed to it? It couldn't possibly work.

Twenty-Mississippi. I wished I *was* in Mississippi. It was warm there. And then I was out of the chamber, and lovely radiant heat was rising from the floor.

"In you go to the next." She shuttled me into the stall next door and closed the glass door behind me before I could turn.

"Don't tense," she shouted through the closed door.

Oh my God. Oh my GOD. I was going to die. I had to get out of here. I looked at the countdown timer on the wall. *Eighty-five seconds.*

There was no way I was going to survive eighty-five seconds. What sort of monster thought up this torture? *Don't tense.*

"Don't tense," she said.

I glared through the glass. I wasn't freaking tensing. How could anyone not tense? It was minus a million degrees. I should be dead. I glanced at the countdown timer. *Eighty seconds.* Only five seconds had passed? How was that even possible?

My breathing accelerated through the mask. I shook like a farm truck's dashboard bobble doll. Did extreme cold slow time?

This was fine. I could step outside whenever I wanted to. I reached toward the door and hesitated. But *did* I want to? Other people had survived ninety seconds. And I only had... *Seventy-five damn seconds to go.* I could do seventy-five—seventy-four seconds.

Time really *did* slow in the cold. It had to be a thing. Had Einstein known? Maybe I should have studied physics instead of getting an MBA. *Don't think about the cold. Relax, relax, relax.*

My neck muscles corded. *No.* It was not humanly possible to relax in this much cold. It was unreasonable. I hated Marla. I hated Frank. They were monsters, sadists.

Breathe. Focus on your breathing. Except even through the mask, the air seemed to be crusting my lungs with ice. The air in my throat wasn't as cold as the rest of me, but it was cold. *Breathe. Breathe.* I watched the timer. *Breathe.*

And then it was finally *five, four, three, two, one.*

I grabbed the door handle and pushed.

It didn't budge.

chapter sixteen

FORTUNE TELLING TABLE

San Francisco, 1968

This fortune telling table is in the form of a Ouija or spirit board, with letters and numbers on its circumference. Artist unknown.

Limbs shaky, I shoved harder on the door.

Nothing happened. I whimpered, the sound freezing in my throat. Had the cold already drained the strength from my muscles? I couldn't even open a simple door. This was where it began. Cold. Numbness. And then death.

Outside the glass, the attendant frowned. She grasped the handle and pulled. The door didn't move.

Marla grabbed it with two hands, leaning back. Desperate, I threw myself against the glass. It refused to yield. The attendant tugged again, her expression frantic. I angled my shoulder toward the door's wooden frame and slammed into it as hard as I could.

A violent tremor ran up my shoulder and into my jaw. The door popped open. I staggered past Marla and against the tile wall. She tumbled to the floor. Mist billowed from the chamber.

She pushed the door closed with one foot and laughed weakly. "Sorry about that. It sticks sometimes. I think the frame's a little crooked."

A *little?* I sank beside her. The tiles were warm, and they felt amazing.

And suddenly, I felt amazing. I was alive, and *life* was incredible. Blood pumped through my limbs. Warm air filled my lungs. It was all I needed. I wanted to roll around on the floor and just soak in the heat.

She pulled an electronic thermometer from the pocket of her white lab coat and aimed it at my head. *BEEP.* "Your temperature's dropped by sixty-one degrees Fahrenheit. Impressive. How do you feel?"

I laughed. "Fantastic." My blood was humming, adrenaline pumping and fizzing in my veins. It was better than my first kiss. It was better than my first trip to Paris. It was better than swimming with dolphins.

Okay, I've never actually swam with dolphins. But I *imagined* it was better than that.

She clambered to her feet. "You can get dressed. I'll let Frank know you're finished here."

"Thanks." I trotted to the locker room and slowly changed back into my normal clothing. It all seemed too hot now, and I slung my Paranormal Museum hoodie over my shoulder.

When I finally emerged into the blue and white waiting area, Frank was there. "How was it?" he asked.

"I don't know if I could force myself to do it again, but it exceeded expectations." I grinned, and he chuckled in response.

"Oh, you'll be back," he said. "Want to see the cryonics facility now?"

I did. Why had I ever been suspicious of the man? He was changing *lives.* And he obviously hadn't killed anyone. He hadn't tried to kill *me.* His utter lack of homicidal intent left me feeling warm and fuzzy. No pun intended. I bit back a giggle.

Frank led me through a series of doors and hallways to the opposite side of the building. He pulled white jumpsuits from a tall, blond-wood cabinet and handed me one. "This is a sterile facility. We already have eight patients. You'll have to put this on."

I zipped myself into the jumpsuit, and I bet it looked amazing on me. Twisting my hair into a loose bun, I snapped on a blue hairnet.

Frank slipped one on as well. He opened a white-painted door, and we walked into a warehouse-like room. Giant upright stainless steel tanks labeled *NITROGEN* emitted cheerful hums.

"We're a bit like a hospital," Frank said. "But all our patients are clinically dead."

"How does it work?" I asked, bouncing on my toes.

"Once the patient is declared clinically dead, they're put on ice and brought here. We replace their blood with Hexlend. It's a fluid that acts like antifreeze. We monitor their temperature with thermocouples throughout the process. Then the patient is put on dry ice and sprayed with liquid nitrogen as their body temperature drops. They're then transferred to the containers you see here and stored in liquid nitrogen."

"And they're... intact?"

"Yes, we're freezing the entire body. So what do you think?"

"I don't think I'd want to come back from the dead." Not if my friends and family were gone. I studied the tall tanks. "I can see why the building inspectors had such trouble with your facility."

"Trouble?" he asked sharply.

"Because it's such a new technology. It's amazing they approved you as fast as they did."

"We're not the first cryonics facility in California." He shifted his weight. "Only the first with cryotherapy attached."

"Which also got approved in record time, at least compared to my museum. Maybe I should add nitrogen tanks," I joked.

He smiled tightly. "Well, that's the tour." He led me out.

We divested ourselves of the jumpsuits and hairnets. Frank saw me to my pickup.

I drove through thick fog back into San Benedetto. Had I imagined the abrupt end to the tour? Had Frank been unusually defensive?

Nah. Life was *good.*

My stomach and the clock on the dash told me it was noon. So instead of going directly to the new museum, I stopped in at the Sunshine Cafe. It was within walking distance of the new museum, and I'd already made friends with the owner, Angelo.

The bell over the door jingled when I walked in, and my spirits lifted even higher. There'd been a bell over the door of my old paranormal museum. We'd decided not to install a bell at the new museum, because it had grown a little annoying. But a bell over someone else's door just seemed charming.

I sat on a sky-blue vinyl counter stool. Angelo, in a green t-shirt and white apron, ambled toward me. "Coffee?"

I nodded. Whistling, I plucked a plastic menu from the metal holder. Frank hadn't been kidding about the after-effects of cryotherapy.

He flipped over the white mug on the counter and filled it with java. "How's your day going?"

"I tried a cryotherapy treatment at that new place down the road."

"You're kidding." He rested a meaty hand on the laminate counter. "What was it like?"

I laughed. "Cold. But I *still* feel amazing."

"Sure. You made it out alive. No wonder you feel like life's sweet mystery."

"What exactly *is* life's sweet mystery?"

"How should I know?" He shrugged. "It's a mystery."

I ordered a grilled cheese sandwich and asked if he could put tomato slices inside. Frank agreed it was a reasonable request and vanished into the kitchen.

Grilled cheese and tomatoes. The thought took me back to my old career—not the part where it had blown up spectacularly, but the quirky good bits.

I'd spent six months in an Islamabad guest house with a massive purple jacaranda out front. The cook had introduced me to grilled cheese and tomato sandwiches with a side of greasy fries. They were a comfort food I hadn't known I'd craved, and I wasn't sure why I wanted them now.

I perused my phone. There weren't any new articles about the museum online, but that was to be expected. And it was a good thing. Getting publicity off Ira's murder came with too much guilt attached.

Angelo returned with my sandwich and fries. "Any word on the dead inspector in your coffin?"

Sarcophagus. I shook my head. "No. Hopefully the police will figure out who put him there."

"I guess it was bound to happen."

"Using my sarcophagus as a body dump?"

"No, one of the inspectors getting offed. You know, after what they've been putting you through."

Had I been complaining *that* much? "It hasn't been so bad," I said. "I mean, the process has been irritating. Really frustrating actually. But they're trying to follow the rules."

"You're lucky then. I hear they've been shaking people down."

Slowly, I set down my phone. "Wait. You're talking about bribes?" *In San Benedetto?*

"That's the word."

I pursed my lips. No one had even hinted at wanting a payoff at the museum. "Were you ever asked to pay them something under the table?"

"Ha. You kidding? None of them would dare. But people talk."

"Like whom?" I frowned and picked up the sandwich. Frank had put some sort of cheese crust on the bread, warm against my fingers.

"I shouldn't say. It's none of my business." The bell at the door jangled. "Hey, Joe." He nodded to an elderly man who'd just entered. Angelo moved to the other end of the counter to chat with him.

My belly knotted. *Payoffs?* Could that be why the cryonics company had been approved so quickly? Frank Frost *had* seemed a little uneasy when I'd commented on the fast approval.

There'd been three men in the inspection department—Ira, Mark, and Ronnie. Were they all in on it? Or had Ira discovered one or more of his staff were on the take, and they'd killed him? Or had Frank gotten rid of an honest inspector, Ira, so he could work with a dishonest one? Or was none of it true at all?

"Something wrong?" Angelo asked.

I stared at the sandwich in my hands. "No." But I wished I'd known this before I'd gone to Frostova this morning.

I finished my sandwich and fries. They were as good as they'd been in Pakistan. Maybe better.

I wiped my greasy fingers then drove to the museum. Herb wasn't around, and I'm ashamed to admit I was relieved. I couldn't put him off forever.

But at least I could ignore the problem today. I spent the next two hours paying bills and playing accountant. They were the least favorite parts of my job.

I studied the phone. I *could* call Frank and just ask him if anyone had asked for a payoff. But he'd just deny it, and I'd miss any tells in his body language.

I pushed back my chair and stood. The direct approach would be better. But my stomach did unpleasant things, and not because of the greasy sandwich. Pushing Frank might cost me a donor. If he was guilty, that wouldn't bother me. But if he was innocent...

Chest weighted, I returned to Frostova. The curving front desk was empty, so I headed toward the cryotherapy rooms.

"Excuse me!" The same, young receptionist hustled toward me, the tails of her lab coat flapping.

I smiled guiltily. "Hi, I seem to have lost my driver's license," I lied. "I think it may have fallen out of my wallet when I was changing. I don't suppose you've found it?"

She adjusted the hair stick in her high bun. "No one's reported finding one to me. Just a minute. I'll ask." She picked up the phone. I settled myself in one of the comfy chairs and studied the marbleized turquoise walls.

She hung up. "No one's found a license in the women's locker room. If you'd like to look for it though, you're welcome to check."

"Thanks. I know the way."

But she wouldn't let me wander on my own, curse her diligence. Making our way to the inner waiting room, she led me to the locker room. I made a show of searching for my license. "Shoot. It's not here either." I straightened from one of the benches.

The attendant's smile was wan. "Losing a license is such a pain. I hope you find it."

"Me too. Hey, is Frank around?" I asked casually.

"I can give him a call, if you like."

"That would be great. Thanks."

We returned to the waiting area. She strolled behind the curving desk and picked up the phone.

A woman's scream echoed off the blue marbleized walls. The attendant's face went ashen, her eyes wide. Unspeaking, we turned and raced down the halls, taking the stairs two at a time.

Tessa backed from Frank's office. Cool air flowed past her, rippling the fabric of her fitted lab coat.

"What is it?" the attendant asked.

The receptionist pointed with a shaking hand. "The window," she croaked.

I strode into Frank's office. The picture window had shattered, bits of safety glass glittering off the wood floor. The curtains billowed.

Stepping to the window, I sucked in a breath. Frank lay still on the pavement below.

chapter seventeen

CREEPY DOLLS

1880s–1920s

This collection of creepy dolls was damaged in a fire at the original paranormal museum. However, it retains its haunting aspects.

It's believed that any object can carry energy. But dolls, which resemble humans and which children emotionally attach to, are particularly susceptible to this phenomenon, enabling spirits to "bond" to them.

"You're not a suspect." Brown eyes serious, Jason studied me from across his desk.

At least we were at his desk and not in an interrogation room. And because of that and because it was Jason, I believed him. Besides, if I was a suspect, he'd be off the case. Conflict of interest.

But that knowledge didn't fill me with relief. The sandwich I'd eaten for lunch curdled in my gut. Maybe it was the memory of Frank, dead on the pavement. Maybe it was the knowledge that a killer had taken two lives and was still out there. Maybe it was Laurel, glowering at me from the next desk.

Or maybe it was something else entirely, something I didn't want to examine too closely. For no reason at all, I thought of my sister, Melanie, and her upcoming Sicilian wedding.

I forced a smile. "That's good to hear."

"The receptionist saw Frank before she left for her lunch break," he continued, "after you'd left Frostova. And you have an alibi from Angelo at the Sunshine Cafe."

"Good," I said, but my heart wasn't in it. "Did you ask Angelo about the bribes?"

He shook his head. "Not over the phone. But I will, later today."

"He did say it was only a rumor." I studied a pencil on his desk. The eraser was a perfect pink cylinder, the lead freshly sharpened. His dark hand rested beside it, his fingernails even crescent moons. How did he get them so perfect? Mine were uneven, all different shapes and sizes.

"You okay?" he asked.

I met his gaze. "Yes. I'm fine." I was just trying not to think of Frank, letting my mind wander over irrelevancies in an attempt at avoidance.

"You couldn't have saved him." Jason leaned closer, his voice gentle.

Was guilt the source of the sick feeling clinging to me? The receptionist and I had rushed into the lot to help Frank. But it had been painfully obvious there was no help to be had. I swallowed. "I know."

"All right," he said. "You can go."

I pushed back my chair and stood. "Thanks. Will I see you later?"

"Not tonight. I'll be working late."

I nodded, my throat thick. I should have known he'd be busy. Now Jason had two murders to solve.

The back of my neck heated, and I glanced over my shoulder at Laurel. She glowered, her blue eyes volcanic.

Correction: *they* had two murders to solve. "I'll see you around then," I said, and I left.

I emerged from the police station into gray afternoon gloom. If anything, the fog had thickened. In my truck, I crept through the dense mist to the museum. I parked in the front lot beside my contractor's battered pickup.

Fresh whorls of soap smeared the new museum's front windows. The white spirals were better than their prior dust and grime, but not by much.

The glass door didn't mute the shrill whir of an electric saw within. Walking past our unlit neon sign, I went inside and strode around the ticket booth to my office.

Before I could reach the wooden door, Chelsea emerged from her office into the small reception area between our rooms. "I thought you'd be here," she said accusingly. In her stylish black, she looked like one of the three fates—the judgey one.

I glanced at Herb's closed door. "Frank Frost died this afternoon," I said.

She took a step backward, her eyes widening. "Oh, no. Our sponsor?"

"Yes." I swallowed. "I had to talk to the police."

"Why?"

"His receptionist and I found Frank's body."

"Oh," she said in a small voice. "I see. I'm sorry. That must have been terrible."

I shook myself. "The Friday of the soft opening, you gave some people a private tour?"

"Yes. I hadn't planned it. That woman from Ladies Aid started showing them around. I thought I should step in and take control. Was that a problem?"

"No," I said. "No problem. Did you leave anyone alone in the hall?"

She straightened. "Of course not."

"You were there the whole time," I pressed, "from one-thirty to three?"

"Roughly. I showed them around, they left, and then I did. Why?"

"It's probably not important." But it let the Town Hall contingent off the hook for stashing the body in the sarcophagus during that time. "Was there something you wanted to talk to me about?"

She brushed back her sleek, dark hair. "What? Oh, yeah. It's that kid, Jordan."

"What about him?"

"He's been trailing after me like a lost puppy and interrupting my work. I can't—"

Jordan stuck his head in the reception area. "Hey. I finished washing the front windows." He glanced at Chelsea, and his face reddened.

Her gaze flicked to the tiled ceiling.

I bit back a sigh. I could send Jordan back to clean them again with water only. But I had a feeling this would involve a good bit of instruction. I'd already been away from my museum work for most of the day.

"How do you feel about research?" I asked him.

The boy stepped into the room, his tennis shoes soft on the thin, gray carpet. "Research?" His eyes narrowed.

"Paranormal research," I clarified, and Chelsea frowned.

"What sort of paranormal research?" he asked.

"Into the life of Paul Foster Case."

His freckled face furrowed. "Who?"

"The guy you drew a mustache on," I clarified.

"Oh." He scratched his head, ruffling his blond hair. "How?"

"Chelsea will help you," I said.

"What?" She crossed her arms and scowled. "Herb's the researcher. I don't have time—"

"We're too small an institution to specialize," I said. "Herb will be assisting you with preservation and documentation. And you... can consider this a chance to broaden your skills into the research arena."

Chelsea studied Jordan, her eyes narrowed. "Hm."

"Maybe start by showing him the artifact you're documenting now," I suggested, backing toward my office door. "Show him how it's done."

"Yeah," he said eagerly. "That'd be cool."

She rubbed her chin.

"Great," I said. "I'll leave you two to it." I hurried into my office and closed the door behind me. For a long moment, I waited, my hand on the knob. There were no shouts of outrage or bangs on my door. Tiptoeing to my desk, I got to work.

I finished all my urgent tasks and guiltily fled the museum before five o'clock. Maybe it was paranoia on my part, but after Frank's death, the fire in the Ladies Aid kitchen seemed less and less like an accident. I wanted to nose around in there before too much was cleaned up.

But I was thwarted by the ladies' devastating efficiency. The kitchen had already been restored, its cabinets glistening with wet paint.

"How'd you get this done so quickly?" I asked, outraged. It took me forever to get contractors and handymen to the museum, and Dieter was *married* to one of my best friends.

My mother arched a brow and leaned one hip against the new stove. "Really, Maddie. You know our resources." Her denim blouse and white jeans were as gleaming as the spic-and-span counters.

"What resources?" I asked. "You said you couldn't get that door fixed."

"The door was different. Mabel's nephew own's a fire and water damage restoration company."

Good to know and moving on. "Did the fire department have any idea how the fire started?"

"It started on the stove." My mother patted the gleaming new state-of-the-art stove—likely a donation. "That's all they said," she continued. "Stovetop fires are quite common."

Frustrated, I walked to the window that had given me so much trouble. "Well, this window was sticking, and..." I studied the twist lock at its base, and my shoulders sagged.

The window hadn't been sticking. It had been locked shut. I'd been too panicked by the fire to think of checking the lock.

I frowned. But the second window I'd tried had opened easily. I stepped sideways. It was locked now. But it hadn't been when the fire had started. "Is this window usually kept unlocked?"

"No. They're both locked whenever they're closed."

"It wasn't locked yesterday," I said.

"Are you sure?"

"I'm sure I didn't unlock it when I raised the window."

My mother's brow furrowed. Angling her head, she tugged on one of her squash blossom earrings. "We haven't had reason to open that window since September. I was certain it was locked. We're very careful with them."

I raised a brow. "You weren't careful with that broken door."

"That's different." Color rose to her cheeks. "We have a sign." She pointed to a three-by-five card taped beside one of the windows. LOCK WHEN CLOSED.

But how long had that window been unlocked? Was that how someone had gotten the body inside?

I shifted uneasily. Kids getting into the museum. Murderers and possibly arsonists sneaking into Ladies Aid. My safe, secure little world was starting to seem a lot less secure.

chapter eighteen

FIRST EDITION THOTH TAROT Cards

Dallas, Texas, 1969

Famed occultist Aleister Crowley collaborated with artist Lady Freida Harris to create the Thoth Tarot deck. These cards are based on the teachings of the Hermetic Order of the Golden Dawn. The society expelled him after he engaged in a magical duel with one of the other members.

The deck wasn't published until after Crowley's death.

"What do you mean the toilet paper roll is a half inch too high?" My nails bit into my palms. Realizing I was clenching my fists, I jammed them into the pockets of my old Paranormal Museum hoodie.

Ronald straightened beside the toilet in the gray-tiled bathroom. "It's a half inch too high. Last year you would have been okay, but this year, the rule is seventeen inches from the center of the roll." The lanky inspector brushed a hand across his red hair. "They're talking about changing it again next year."

My neck corded. *Are you kidding me?* "How does an inch higher make it harder to reach?"

I knew it was a useless question. Logic had nothing to do with it. But I couldn't help myself. Every time I thought I'd done what a building inspector wanted, they came up with more demands. It wasn't fair.

Ronald grimaced and made a note on his clipboard. "Sorry. Those are the rules."

My skull detonated in impotent fury, vaporized, and reconstituted itself. Fortunately, I was the only one who noticed the explosion.

I trailed the inspector to the door of the museum's tiny employee kitchen. There wasn't enough space inside for two people. He squinted at a bare light bulb over the metal sink. "This is the wrong kind of eco-bulb."

"I'll get a different one," I ground out. That, at least, would be easy enough.

He hesitated. "I heard you found Frank Frost's body."

I blinked at the change of subject. "Me and one of his employees."

He tucked his clipboard beneath his slender arm. "They're saying it's connected to Ira's murder."

"Who's saying that?"

He shrugged. "Everyone. It makes sense, doesn't it? Two murders so close together in one small town? And Ira did the Frostova inspection."

"We don't know when Ira was killed," I said slowly. Though it was a good bet it had happened around the time he'd disappeared. "Did you know Frank Frost?"

Ronald shook his head. "I wasn't involved with his inspection." He opened a cupboard beneath the sink and squatted, studying the mini water heater there. "It's not a good feeling being part of a murder investigation. Everyone's looking at us and wondering."

"Wondering what?"

He stood, and his expression hardened. "Nothing. Never mind."

Ronald finished his inspection. He left me with a list of niggly things to fix and a promise to return next week for a final inspection.

I stormed into my office, did *not* slam the door, and I called Dieter. The contractor promised to pick up the to-fix list when he got to the museum tomorrow.

I hung up. The phone rang beneath my fingertips, and I answered. "Did you forget something Dieter?"

"Uh, Maddie?" an unfamiliar male voice asked.

I frowned. "Yes. Who's calling?"

"This is Mike, from the San Benedetto Times."

"Oh," I said flatly. "Hi. What's up?" It was unlikely he was angling for positive press for the museum. Leaning back in my executive chair, I braced myself.

"Is it true you discovered Frank Frost's body yesterday?"

My jaw tightened. I forced myself to relax. "Yes."

"What were you doing at Frostova?"

"Frostova's a sponsor—they've been a sponsor of the museum," I hedged.

"Yeah. I heard you had an appointment earlier, got a cold treatment, then came back and found the body."

My gaze flicked toward the tiled ceiling. If he knew so much, why was he calling? "That's correct."

"Why'd you go back? Did you forget something?"

"I thought I'd lost my driver's license when I was getting my cryotherapy." I hated lying, but now I was stuck with the fib. I fiddled with a loose pen, which had run out of ink.

I tossed it in the wire garbage bin beside my desk. "I went back for it, heard a woman scream, and the receptionist and I ran to see what had happened. That's when we found Frank."

"Huh." He managed to infuse the syllable with a career's-worth of disbelief. "So a body was found in your sarcophagus at an event Frank sponsored. And then Frank was killed, and you were one of the people who found him."

Thank you, Captain Obvious. "That is correct." I'd learned when it comes to the press and the police to keep my responses short and succinct.

"Do you think there's a connection between your museum and the murders?"

I swiveled my chair toward the high windows, gray with fog. "Aside from the one you just stated, no."

"Who do you think killed Frank Frost?"

"I have no idea."

He snorted.

"You should ask Detective Laurel Hammer," I said brightly. "I believe she's one of the investigating officers."

"Yeah, no thanks. What about—?"

"Sorry," I caroled. "Gotta go." I hung up. Elbows on the desk, I buried my head in my hands. Had I said too much?

Of course I had.

But I couldn't take it back. So I did other things.

I emailed the agenda for the next board meeting to the members. I sent the final copy of our online ad to the upcoming Harvest Festival, which we were sponsoring. And then I drove to the Bell and Brew to meet Harper for lunch.

My friend had already claimed a booth near a giant, copper beer vat. I slid onto the red bench across from her. "Hey." A tall glass of iced tea stood beside my napkin, and I smiled. Harper knew me well.

"How'd the inspection go?" She adjusted the collar of her forest-green turtleneck, shifting the slim gold necklace around the collar.

"There are a few tiny things to fix, but nothing major." *Stupid lightbulb. Stupid toilet paper roll.*

"That's good news."

I studied the menu, though I already knew I'd be ordering a blue-cheese burger. I always ordered the blue-cheese burger. Was I in a rut? "Good news is something we all need."

She sipped her tea. "All?"

"Ronnie—Ronald implied things are getting uncomfortable for the inspection department."

"Of course it's uncomfortable. More than uncomfortable." Her dark brows lowered. "Their chief inspector was murdered."

"Which makes them all suspects, especially if there's corruption involved."

Harper banged her iced tea on the table. Brown liquid slopped over the edge of the glass. "Corruption?"

I lowered my menu. "It's classic blame-the-victim mentality. Ira was murdered, ergo he must have done something wrong to cause it. Normally I'd discount that sort of suspicion. But what if it's true?"

She adjusted the collar of her turtleneck. "That doesn't make sense. If Ira was killed because he was taking bribes, who killed him? One of his victims? It'd be easier to pay the bribe, and if not, to report him."

"Ira was one of the inspectors for Frostova. And now Frank Frost is dead too."

She glanced around the crowded restaurant. "If you're implying Frank paid off Ira," she said in a low voice, "why kill Ira? And why kill Frank?" She pointed at my chest, and I felt an arrow of heat strike my breastbone.

I rubbed the spot. "Mark Spicer was involved in that inspection too. What if he was crooked and Ira found out?"

"You can't throw around accusations like that," she hissed.

"I'm not throwing them around. I'm talking to you."

Harper sat back in the booth and grimaced. "And I'm getting defensive. Sorry." She blew out her cheeks, her full lips pursing. "Okay. It's possible. Of course it's possible. The fact is..." She met my gaze. "I'm having second thoughts about being a town councilor."

My head jerked backward. Second thoughts? Harper was too responsible for second thoughts. Unlike some people (*ha*), she looked before leaping. "Why?"

"When I ran, I was just thinking about San Benedetto. My town. *Our* town. But I was approached by someone—let's just say high up—who laid out a path for me to go higher, into the state legislature." She made a face.

"And you don't want to?" It sounded like an amazing opportunity for Harper and the state.

"I was flattered, of course. I love California. But the path they laid out... It wouldn't matter what I thought or what I did. The expectation was I'd vote with my party, regardless. I'd just be another proxy. A proxy with a lot of benefits, and a lot of opportunities to... benefit more. It felt greasy. It *is* greasy."

"What sort of benefits?" I asked, the skin on my arms crawling.

A glass crashed, and I glanced over my shoulder. But all I saw was the back of the wooden booth.

"Some of them are silly," she said, not meeting my gaze. "Do what you're told, and you get a nice office. Don't, and you're in the basement. Did you know state legislators get their cars washed and filled with gas every time they park at the capitol? They don't have to even pay for the gas. But there were other things..."

Harper shook her head. "I told her I wasn't interested. She threatened—well implied—the party would fund my opposition at the next election."

"What do they care about San Benedetto?" I exploded. "We're tiny. We're nothing." This was crazy. Wasn't anywhere safe from corruption?

Her smile was wan. "The town's a source of income. Look at all the development that's going on. People are making money off it. And I hate to say it, but those people are donating to politicians who make sure the developers get the land they want at the price they want. And that's only one piece of it. I don't know what's going on in our inspection department. Ira had a reputation as a straight shooter. Maybe he did uncover something he shouldn't have."

Harper jammed her index finger onto the table. "But I won't—I *can't* make accusations without real evidence. This is all supposition, and it's wrong and unfair. There are good people working for San Benedetto. People who are trying to do the right thing. I won't smear them."

A waitress appeared at our table. "Can I take your order?"

Harper smiled up at her, and it was the smile of a politician, slick and fake. But Harper wasn't a politician. She was honest and honorable. She did things because they were right, not because they might earn votes.

But this was the same Harper, her gold earrings modest, her turtleneck and slacks neat and professional. She was one of my best friends. She hadn't changed.

The stained glass lamp above our table tinted Harper's dark hair in unnatural reds and oranges. "I'd like the chicken and apple salad," my friend said.

Screw the bridesmaid dress. I ordered the blue-cheese burger. Murder trumped diets.

The waitress departed. And I thought of Harper's smile. Nausea swam in my gut.

I wanted to say more about the inspectors. Now, I wasn't sure how.

"How are things at the museum?" Harper asked.

Relieved, I seized on the change of topic. We talked about the museum, and the grand opening, and how Jordan was working out.

And then after lunch, I drove to my mother's ranch house. Her Lincoln SUV was parked in the driveway. I knocked on the door, then tried the knob. It was open. Pensive, I walked inside. "Mom?"

"In here," she called from the kitchen.

I walked into her kitchen, and a knot eased between my shoulders. *Home.* Gray, granite island and counters. Distressed cupboards with missing cabinet doors, cheerful red plates and mugs on full display.

My mother stood at the kitchen island rolling out dough. She set the rolling pin aside. Brushing flour from her hands, she wiped them on her checked apron.

"What are you doing here?" she asked. "I thought you'd be at the museum. Are you ready for your board meeting?"

I adjusted the *v* of my hoodie. "Of course I am." I didn't have much to report, and I'd already emailed all the financials to the museum board.

I hesitated. I'd planned to ask her about the rumors of corruption at Town Hall. But if I told her, I'd have to ask her not to tell Ladies Aid. And that wasn't fair, not with her in the midst of a recall. The ladies would be outraged if they found out my mom knew something spicy and hadn't shared.

"You're not nervous?" she asked.

"Why would I be nervous?" I stepped backward, and my hip struck a smoke-tiled counter.

She shrugged. "You're here."

Just ask her. But I couldn't do it. "I smelled cookies."

She nodded toward cookies shaped like pumpkins and ghosts cooling on wire racks. "Help me frost them, and you can have one."

It seemed a little early for Halloween cookies, but her spice cookies were famous throughout the hallowed halls of Ladies Aid. "Only one?"

She gave me a pointed look. "I thought you wanted to lose weight before your sister's wedding?"

"That's not until March," I protested.

Her mouth flattened. "And you'll need to tell Melanie soon if Jason's coming or not. She needs to know. *Is he coming?*"

Warmth crept across my cheeks. "I, ah, haven't asked him yet."

"What?" She cocked her head. "Why not? He's going to need to request time off work."

"Yeah." I shifted my weight. "I mean, it's a big ask, isn't it? To take all that time off?"

My mother crossed her arms and faced me fully. "So you ask, and if he can't, he says *no*. What's the problem?"

"Asking him to my sister's Sicilian wedding just seems like a big step," I hedged.

"You've been seeing each other for some time now. You two are exclusive, aren't you?"

My face grew hotter. "Yes, of course."

"You and Jason aren't having problems?" Her blue eyes turned serious.

"No, everything's fine." We had a nice, adult relationship. I rallied. "We're good."

"So what's the issue?"

"There's no issue. It just seems a little... much."

"Why?" she asked reasonably.

"I don't know. You're right. It's no big deal. I'll just ask him and see what he says." So why did I suddenly find it so hard to breathe?

chapter nineteen

SAN BENEDETTO POLICE ARE *investigating the death of Mr. Frank Frost, whose body was found after an apparent fall from his office on the third floor of Frostova, a cryonics company.*

Maddie Kosloski, whose paranormal museum was being sponsored by Frostova, called 911 at about one o'clock PM, after she and two Frostova employees discovered the body. The death is being investigated as a homicide.

Anyone with information about this incident should call Detective Laurel Hammer at the San Benedetto Police Department.

I set the newspaper on my desk and looked up at Leo. "Thanks," I said, not quite meaning it. I loved that Leo thought beyond his museum to-do list. But the article was depressing

My assistant shrugged, his black leather jacket squeaking. He leaned forward in his chair. "It's not exactly publicity, but I thought you'd want to see it. Not to be cold, but what's going to happen to the sponsorship?"

"I don't know," I said, numb. And contacting Frostova to ask was out of the question. I'm nosy, but I draw the line at crass. "And it's not cold. It's realistic. But I think we'll have to assume it's off and work from there."

Leo nodded.

"Don't worry," I said with a false laugh. "You'll still get paid."

Leo was working on an augmented reality app for our exhibits. It was the first chance I'd had to give him a project that worked toward his talents. I was determined to see it through.

Also, the AR concept was cool. Guests could point their tablet or phone at an exhibit to bring it to life onscreen. Leo was determined to make it spooky.

One corner of Leo's mouth crooked upward. "I know I will. I'm not worried about me. I guess..." He looked around my office, its shelves cluttered with books and paranormal artifacts. "I just want the museum to succeed."

"It will." It had to. "How are you and Chelsea getting on?"

Leo's cheeks flushed. "Fine."

I raised a brow.

He sat back in his chair and scuffed one booted foot on the gray carpet. His smile was rueful. "She knows her stuff. More than I do."

"You were always meant for more than this museum. It's okay if she's more knowledgeable about managing artifacts."

He lowered his head. His carob-colored eyes bored into mine.

I laughed shortly. "And yes, I've been feeling a little defensive about that too. But my specialty is marketing and promotion. It makes sense for me to focus there."

"You're not the only one," he said.

"What do you mean?"

"Herb's still smarting after the Grand Opening."

I frowned. "What's going on with him?"

"Didn't you see? He was showing off his knowledge to some reporters and got buzzed by a wasp."

Eeesh. That explained the flailing. Herb was terrified of all stinging insects. But whatever embarrassment Herb had suffered at the soft opening, everyone else must have forgotten it by now. The shock of a body falling from our sarcophagus had overshadowed the rest of the evening.

Leo rose. "You ready for the board meeting?"

You too? "Sure. It's no big deal. The board's a friendly crowd."

"Cool. I'll have a beta app ready to test next week." He sauntered from my office.

I drummed my fingers on the desk. I checked my calendar. I checked my emails. And then I drove to Frostova.

In his newspaper article, Mike hadn't drawn the connection I'd feared between the murders and the museum. But a connection was there, however tenuous. At least, I liked to think it was tenuous. Still, I couldn't ignore it.

But when I arrived, Frostova's blue glass front doors were locked. I rattled the handle uselessly and stepped back in the swirling fog.

"Can I help you?" a woman asked from behind me.

I jumped a little and turned. Frank's executive assistant, Tess, stood there in jeans and a fisherman's sweater.

I pressed a hand to my chest. "Sorry. You startled me."

She didn't smile. "I didn't mean to. Can I help you?" she repeated. Moisture glistened on her loose, brown hair.

"I came here on Tuesday looking for my driver's license," I lied, and this time I didn't feel a twinge of guilt. That worried me a little. I *should* feel guilty. Was I changing too?

"I thought I'd dropped it in the cryotherapy locker room," I continued. "Now I wonder if I didn't somehow drop it in Frank's office."

She shook her head. "The police don't want anyone going in there. It's locked up."

"It looks like the whole building is."

Tess nodded. "Except for the cryotherapy spa. Everything's still running inside for our cryogenics clients. But the office operations have stopped until the board decides what to do next."

She looked up at the building. The top floor was lost in mist. "I'm not needed."

"I'm sorry," I said. "To lose your job and your colleague at the same time...." I knew that untethered, unemployed feeling. "Were you and Frank close?" I asked quietly.

She exhaled through pursed lips. "He was a good man. We didn't socialize outside the office, but he was a good person."

A part of me hated that that was true. I wanted Frank to be a bad guy, someone who'd deserved what he'd gotten. But sometimes bad things happened to people who did all the right things. "Who could have done this to him?"

Tess met my gaze. "I don't know. I've been wracking my brain trying to think..." She shook her head. "I must have been at lunch when it happened. Frank did *not* jump from that window. He wasn't depressed or suicidal. Someone pushed him. But he didn't have any appointments. I don't know who..." She swallowed and looked away, blinking rapidly.

"Did he have conflicts with anyone?"

"Like with that dead building inspector?" She laughed hollowly. "That's what the police asked me. And no, he didn't."

"Could someone have gotten to his office with no one noticing?" I asked.

The executive assistant nodded. "Of course. You saw what it was like. The workers who manage the vats don't come through the front. They all work in the back. Same with the spa employees. They have a separate entrance, like their clients. The cryonics operation doesn't get visitors. The receptionist you met was a temp. She's not even here five days a week. She went to lunch, and..." She shrugged.

"And the front doors weren't locked while she was gone?"

"Why would they be? We're off the beaten path." She motioned toward the empty field bordering the parking lot. "There's nothing to steal."

"No cameras?"

"There are cameras in the cryonics storage area. That's all."

It should have been enough. My mother rarely locked her front door either. The world had changed, but our habits had not. And that was a mistake.

"I keep thinking about that cursed sarcophagus," she said suddenly.

I stiffened. "Oh?" But at least she knew the difference between a coffin and an Egyptian sarcophagus.

"I can't stop thinking about it," she said. "I was at the soft opening, you know."

I hadn't known. I hadn't seen her there. But I'd been preoccupied.

She cleared her throat. "I read about that curse that dooms anyone who disturbs the tomb."

"The tomb was disturbed long ago."

"But that curse," she continued. "And that man, wrapped up like a mummy, just like the curse warned."

The actual curse hadn't doomed people to become mummies per se. Just to die horribly. The mummy part had been implied, mostly by me. But in the paranormal museum business, taking a few liberties with a story was par for the course.

"It would have taken a lot of strength to shove Frank through that window," she said. "Almost supernatural strength." She colored.

Supernatural? She couldn't think... a mummy had done it? My hands dropped to my sides. Me and my stupid liberties. "You don't think...?"

"No." She shook her head. "Of course not. A mummy didn't kill Frank. I *know* a mummy didn't kill Frank. But I can't stop *imagining* one did. It's like the imp of the perverse. That thing you know you shouldn't think about, but you can't let it go. Sorry. I'm not making sense." Turning, she strode to a blue Accord and got inside the car.

Thoughtful, I returned to my pickup. Would it have taken much force to push Frank through a window? I imagined it would depend on the window. And in new commercial buildings, they should be fairly sturdy. Shouldn't they?

It was the sort of question I might ask a building inspector. I started my truck and cruised through the parking lot. A black RAM pickup—one of the big ones—started up behind me. Its automatic lights flashed on.

I checked my own lights and discovered I hadn't turned them on. I'd probably driven all the way here with them off, and I grimaced. That was the challenge with driving vintage—no conveniences like auto wipers and electric windows. I turned onto the road and glanced in my rearview.

The truck loomed, filling the mirror. There was a horrible grinding of metal, and I lurched forward.

Another challenge with vintage? No shoulder belts. My forehead slammed against the wheel.

chapter twenty

HAUNTED GRAPE PRESS

San Benedetto, circa 1900

*This grape press once belonged to the Constantino family and is connect-
ed to the murders of Alcina Constantino and her lover, Luigi Rotta, in 1922.*

I did not black out.

But I wished I had. Pain splintered my forehead. I whiplashed against
the seat.

A row of grapevines sprouted through the fog in front of my bumper.
I cursed and swerved, overcompensating. My wheels bumped, and my
pickup crashed nose down in a ditch.

The RAM blasted past.

Heart pounding, I gripped the pickup's broad wheel. And then I scrambled for the pen in my glove compartment and scrawled the RAM's
license plate number on my palm.

I swore some more, because it made me feel better, and I clambered
from the truck. At least vintage vehicles were built to last. Paint was
scratched off the rear bumper, damp with fog, but the only thing dented
was my license plate.

Climbing back inside, I sat there for a long moment, gripping the wheel.
Then I put the pickup in reverse and drove out of the ditch with only
some minor wheel spinning. I parked on the side of the road and called
Jason. It went to voicemail.

"Hi," I said. "A black RAM pickup just ran me off the road. I guess it was a hit and run, since he rammed my bumper. No pun intended. Ah... I got the license." I recited it. "I'm okay, but... just thought I should report it." I hesitated. "Hope you're having a good day. Bye."

I rubbed the back of my neck and called Harper.

"Hey," she said. "What's up?"

I started the ignition. "I'm headed to Town Hall. I thought I'd drop in if you were there."

"I'm not," she said. "I'm at my office."

I grimaced. In a town as small as San Benedetto, town council was a part-time gig. Harper would be busy with clients. "I'll catch you later then."

"Is something wrong? You sound funny."

"No, no." I pulled onto the road. "I just had a question for the inspection department about windows."

"Oh. Okay. You're not nervous about your board meeting, are you?"

Why did people keep asking me about that meeting? I'd chosen everyone on the board. They were all friendly toward me and the museum, and they were on the board to support it. "No, I'm ready."

"If you're sure," she said doubtfully.

I frowned. "Of course I'm sure." I *had* prepared for the meeting.

"Well if you need any help, let me know."

"Thanks," I said, drawing out the word. What did she think was going to happen at the meeting? A ritual application of thumbscrews? "I'll talk to you later."

We said our goodbyes. I drove to Town Hall and wandered its modern corridors to the inspection department. Naturally, since I didn't have an appointment, all the building inspectors were out.

I stared at their office's locked metal door, which was no doubt up to the latest fire code. Maybe I could find what I needed online?

"Maddie?" Head cocked, Janice Walsh clacked toward me on her mid-sized heels. "What are you doing here?" The young woman wore a hickory-colored business suit. She clutched a tablet computer in one hand.

"Looking for information about commercial windows."

"I'd have thought your windows were already installed," she said, angling away from me. "Is there a problem?"

"Not for the museum," I said quickly. "For new builds. I don't suppose you know if they have strength requirements?"

"I know they do, but not what the requirements are. There's a website with the code, but I doubt you'll understand the answer there. No offense, but the requirements are fairly complex and depend on a lot of different factors."

"No offense taken." I shifted my weight on the laminate floor.

Her mouth pursed. "Why are you interested?"

"Frank Frost was shoved through a third-floor office window. I was curious about how difficult that would be."

Janice's expression stilled. "Oh."

"I'm sorry. Did you know him?"

She blinked rapidly. "Not well. Not really. We met for the first time at your soft opening."

"I suppose you managed the permitting for his facility."

"I signed off on it, yes. But I never met the man. Not until your museum party."

"Was there anything unusual about the Frostova permit?" I asked.

Janice pressed the tablet computer to her chest, flattening the folds of her brownish suit. "For a cryonics facility and spa? It was all new to me. But there weren't any problems that I know of, if that's what you're asking."

"I'm not sure what I'm asking." I smiled bitterly. "Sorry. Frank was a museum supporter. I'm just trying to make sense of all this. First Ira, then Frank..."

She paled. "Yes. Well. We're all trying to make sense of it."

"Were you and Ira very close?"

She straightened. Twin spots of color darkened her cheeks. "What do you mean?"

"I just thought... since he confided to you about Wynnona..."

"We were colleagues. Ira was always professional. And now if you'll excuse me..." She turned and hurried down the hall, her heels cracking on the faux wood flooring.

I stared after her. I didn't think I'd imagined her reaction. It had seem ed... defensive. *Could* Janice and him have had something going?

My cell phone rang, and I tugged it free of the rear pocket of my jeans. *Jason.* Smiling, I answered. "Hey."

"I got your message. Are you okay?"

I rubbed the back of my neck. "All I got from the encounter was a dented license plate." *And a future visit to a chiropractor.*

"The driver rear-ended you?"

"Yeah. Fortunately, I wasn't going very fast." I leaned one shoulder against the adobe-colored wall. "I was on the road leaving Frostova."

"Frostova," Jason said flatly.

I winced. "Frank was a donor." And I was prevaricating, hoping the statement would be enough to excuse my presence. I straightened off the wall. "And I was being nosy."

He sighed. "Gotcha. Did you get a look at the person driving?"

"No. Why? Did I get the plate wrong?"

"No," he said. "Not wrong. The truck you described was reported stolen."

chapter twenty-one

ZOLTAN FORTUNE TELLING MACHINE

Massachusetts, 1967

This Zoltan Fortune Teller comes from a long line of fortune telling machines. To get your fortune, deposit a quarter, put the phone receiver to your ear, and press one of the zodiac buttons on the front. The crystal ball will light, and you will receive your fortune. May it be a good one!

I hate meetings. Most are a waste of breath. So I'm militant about having an actual purpose and goals on the rare occasions I attend any.

But I hadn't run a meeting in a long time. When it had been just me and Leo managing the original paranormal museum, there hadn't been much call for it. And I guess all those people asking me if I was ready for this one had gotten to me a little.

There was no reason this morning's confab shouldn't flow smoothly. There were only five people on the board including myself, and they were all friendlies.

I looked around the colorful, sixties-era fortune telling table. Neatly folded Paranormal History Museum hoodies covered the all-seeing eye in the table's center.

Adele's father, Roy Nakamoto, braced his elbows on the round table. He studied our financials, his shirt sleeves rolled to his elbows. As a vineyard owner and entrepreneur, he had a wealth of local business and tourism experience. Light from the pastel-crystal chandelier tinted the gray strands in his hair pink.

Likewise, Penny, from the Wine Visitor's Bureau, was a cornerstone of local tourism. The plump woman frowned down at the financials at well, her wine-bottle earrings jiggling.

Harriet, from the Historical Association, wandered the room. She studied the cards describing the exhibits—vintage spirit boards, first edition Tarot cards, and a Zoltan fortune telling machine. The faint scent of peppermint schnapps trailed in her wake. The gray-haired woman adjusted her spectacles and peered at the turbaned Zoltan.

Sam Levitt, a local lawyer, was a weedy-looking man in wrinkled khakis and a gray, button-up shirt. His youthful face was carved in a hangdog expression, or at least what I could see of it was. He sat at the table reading on his phone.

Straightening on my wooden chair, I checked the time on my own phone and cleared my throat. "Shall we start?"

Harriet, in a yellow blouse and brown skirt, ambled to her empty chair and sat. "By all means. The Association of California Historical Associations is having a Zoom meeting at noon. I don't want to be late."

"And I've got a client meeting," Sam said.

"So let's talk museum," Harriet continued brightly. "Will the museum be represented at the Harvest Festival?"

"Yes, we're one of the sponsors." I tried to look sanguine, but the festival started this weekend. Had I forgotten to do anything for it? "Thanks for coming everyone, and thanks for agreeing to be on the museum board. As you can see from our financials, so far we're on budget."

"That's a lot of events in a short period of time." Roy Nakamoto looked up. "I hope you're not stretched too thin. What about the grand opening? I understood that Frostova was one of the main sponsors of that event."

I nodded. "I don't know if they're going to be able to fulfill their pledge. I think we have to assume they won't, however."

"Their pledge was half the budget for the grand opening," Roy said.

"Yes," I said. "We'll either have to scale back or find funds somewhere else."

"Do you have any prospects?" Harriet tilted her head. Her thin silvery glasses chain caught in the collar of her pale yellow blouse.

"Not yet," I admitted. "And I'm open to suggestions."

"It's a quandary." Penny tugged on one of her wine-bottle earrings. "On the one hand, that body in the sarcophagus provided so much press, a grand opening is almost superfluous. On the other hand, it would be a shame not to capitalize on that momentum. And yes, murder is awful, and it's horrible that this happened at all. But the story went global."

"My aunt called from Okinawa to make sure I hadn't been murdered," Roy said glumly.

Sam looked up from his phone. "I'm more concerned about the legal ramifications. This could leave the museum open to a lawsuit."

"A lawsuit?" I said weakly. "How? No one from the museum put Ira in the sarcophagus. And it wasn't even on museum grounds."

"But it was a museum event," Sam said. "And this is California. Have you been contacted by any of Ira's relatives?"

"His ex-wife stopped by," I admitted.

He set his phone down, covering the table's letter X. "I hope you didn't say anything to her that might have been an admission of liability. *I'm sorry for your loss* could be enough."

My hands spasmed. *What?* "I don't remember. But I probably did say something like that. I mean, it's what one says." Had I put the museum at risk of a lawsuit?

"What did she want?" the lawyer asked.

"To gloat," I said, "I think. Apparently there was no love lost between her and Ira."

"A pity she was in Florida when he died," Penny smoothed the front of her *Time for Wine* t-shirt. "If she was the killer, she couldn't profit from his death with a lawsuit."

"How do you know she was in Florida?" I asked, surprised.

Penny smiled. "My dear, their divorce was big news in San Benedetto, especially after the rumors of Ira's infidelity."

"But we're not even sure when he died," I protested. "I mean, we know when he was put in the sarcophagus—roughly, but—"

"That's true," Penny said. "His ex *might* have been able to kill him. But she couldn't have put him in the sarcophagus. She was in Florida."

"I don't suppose you know who Ira was unfaithful with?" I asked. Or was it *whom* he was unfaithful with?

GD slunk into the room. The black cat hopped onto a glass display case and from there to the top of the Zoltan machine.

Roy cleared his throat. "Maybe we should stay on task."

My face warmed. "Sorry. You're right."

"Nonsense," Harriet said. "Of course Maddie wants to clear up this murder. The museum's involved, even if only tangentially." She smiled. "I suppose you've been questioning all the suspects. Who are they?"

"Well," I said, glancing at the lawyer. "Keep this to yourselves, but there have been rumors of some, er, corruption in Ira's department."

Harriet sucked in her breath. "Bribes? Did any of the building inspectors ask you for money?"

GD meowed.

"No," I said. "And I would have reported it if one had. Frostova's inspection moved fairly quickly, and then Frank Frost was killed..."

Harriet's eyes widened behind her glasses. "You think a building inspector killed Frank to keep him from talking?"

"I don't know," I said. "But there are only two inspectors in that department now. Both want Ira's job."

"Which alone could be a motive," Harriet said. "It may have nothing to do with corruption."

Roy frowned.

"And then there were those rumors of Ira's infidelity," I continued. "His ex-wife implied his, er, paramour was someone at Town Hall." *Janice?* Working in permitting, she'd have worked closely with the inspectors.

"And passion can lead to murder," Harriet murmured.

"With everything that's going on to open the museum, is this the best use of your time?" Roy asked gently.

I felt myself flush. "Sorry. What I really wanted to talk to you about today is our strategic plan. That's page four of your packet."

We worked through the strategic plan. As I'd hoped, my board provided several excellent suggestions.

I closed the meeting, gave everyone a hoodie, and walked them to the exit through the gift shop. Harriet, Sam, and Penny hurried off. Adele's father lingered.

Roy rested an elbow on the old-fashioned brass register. He slung his hoodie over one shoulder. "Maddie, I didn't want to say anything in front of the others, but I'm a little concerned about this murder."

"Honestly, the only connection Ira had to the museum was his killer put his body in our sarcophagus. The police don't seem to consider anyone at the museum a suspect."

"That's not what I meant. I meant you."

"I'm not a suspect either."

Roy grimaced. "Look. You're a smart woman, and there's no one better to manage this museum."

My stomach wormed. "But?"

"But you have a tendency to get distracted by true crime. I can't entirely blame you this time, since the body was in our sarcophagus. But there's a lot riding on this museum. Not only is the whole town watching, but as Harriet said, the attention's gone global. And now with one of our patrons falling through..."

"The museum's operating plan is on track."

"Except we still haven't received a final inspection approval."

"No," I said. "But that's in the works."

"And some of your employees have... not exactly complained, but mentioned you haven't been giving your full focus to the museum."

I stiffened. "Have they?" Only three employees could have noticed I'd been out more than usual—Chelsea, Herb, and Leo. And I knew Leo and Herb hadn't narced on me.

His smile was lopsided. "The good news is they care about the museum's success too. Finding an alternate sponsor for the grand opening would go a long way to show you're on top of things. Maybe a larger corporation with operations outside the town?"

I forced a smile. The criticism stung. But I hadn't asked Roy to be on the board to tell me how wonderful I was. I'd asked him and the others to join up so they could stopgap my weaknesses. "You're right. I'll get on that."

He clapped my shoulder. "I know you will. You've done a great job pulling this together. I'm sure the grand opening will be just as quality." He ambled out the glass door.

I sagged against the counter. A *new sponsor?* The grand opening was in just over a month. And big corporations took time to decide on how to spend their marketing bucks. Time I shouldn't have been wasting these last three days.

Dullness settled in my chest. I'd screwed up. Talking to the widow, playing detective when I should have been looking for a new sponsor. I'd screwed up. Big time.

chapter twenty-two

Spiritoscope

Pennsylvania, 1856

This spiritoscope was designed by a chemistry professor, Dr. Robert Hare. It's goal was to not only aid mediums, but to prevent trickery. He created as many as six versions of this mechanical device.

This spiritoscope includes a disk imprinted with the alphabet for communication by letter. The medium was unable to see its operation. Hare reasoned this could validate the message, because the mediums would have no control over it.

The spiritoscope was eventually simplified by other spiritual seekers into the planchette and the Ouija board.

There's a special skill set involved in asking for money.

I don't have it.

Charging for tickets, selling monthly paranormal "boxes" online, even flogging ghost hunts I could do. But asking for donations and sponsors curdled my gut. Unfortunately, it was also a critical part of my new job.

I hated it.

"Oh, yeah," the woman on the other end of the line said. "I think I did hear about your museum. There was a real body in that Egyptian coffin?"

Sarcophagus. I sagged lower in my executive chair. Watery sunlight leaked through the afternoon fog blocking the high windows. I reached across my desk and switched on the metallic desk lamp.

"That was us," I said. "But we had nothing to do with the body. Someone snuck it into the sarcophagus as...." A prank? To shift the blame to the museum? "...a way to dump a body," I ended.

"Most people just leave them in airport parking," the woman said. "But I guess you don't have an airport in San Benedetto."

"No," I said slowly. *Take control of the conversation.* I glanced down at my notes. "The museum has already received nationwide and international press. As a sponsor of our grand opening this Halloween, you'll not only receive access to paranormal and Halloween enthusiasts, but your company's name will be included in all the press for the event. That includes press releases, our website, and on all advertising—including a banner at the event itself."

"I think it's a wonderful idea."

I straightened in my chair. "You do? I mean, that's terrific. What can I do to move this along?"

"I already have the information you emailed. I'll shoot it up the chain and recommend we do this next year."

I pressed my lips tight. Next *year*? "Ah... That's great, but the grand opening is this year, this Halloween."

She laughed lightly. "But I'm sure you'll be having another event next Halloween, won't you?"

"We'll be hyping the entire month of October."

"Even better. I'm sure we can work out a sponsorship then."

My mouth went dry. "Thank you. I'd hate for you to miss out on this particular opportunity with our grand opening though. As I said, press interest in the museum is high."

Because of the murder. I winced. I was *not* going to pitch murder as an advertising benefit. "Our recent expansion has transformed the paranormal museum into a fun and educational attraction."

"I'm sorry, but there's no way I can get approval that quickly."

I rubbed my forehead. My fingers came away slick, and I wiped them on my jeans. "I understand. We'll be thrilled to have your company as a sponsor next year. What additional information do you think you'll need?"

"I can't think of a thing, but if I do, I'll let you know."

"Great. Enjoy the rest of your day."

We said our goodbyes, and I hung up. I dropped backward in my executive chair. It swayed sickeningly.

Any other day, I'd have been thrilled with the call. Finding sponsors and donors took time and relationship building. Laying up a sponsorship for next year was a win. But I needed a sponsor *now*.

And the more I beat myself up and freaked myself out, the lower the odds that I could find one. I tossed my pen on my desk. It rolled to a halt beside a stack of bills. I needed a break.

My office door blasted open. "Am I, or am I not the curator of this collection?" Herb demanded, his coke-bottle spectacles flashing.

What now? "You are the curator," I said.

He jammed his hands on his narrow hips, rucking up his tweed jacket. "Then why are Chelsea and that boy researching Paul Foster Case? And why won't you send me to the curation class I requested?"

I rubbed the bridge of my nose. "They're doing research because I was running out of things for Jordan to clean. And he needed something to do that would engage his brain. And you haven't been around. Where—?"

"You mean you don't want to supervise that boy." Herb folded his arms.

"That too," I said. "What's the problem?"

"The problem is I'm the researcher."

And he was feeling insecure. That was something I understood too. "And you already know everything there is to know about Paul Foster Case and that exhibit."

"So why—?"

"You're right," I said. "I should have brought you into it. The fact is, teenage boys are one of our key target markets. We need to know what *they* find interesting about the paranormal so we can be sure to include it."

His hands dropped to his sides. "You're saying the boy's a test subject."

"Ah..." Putting it that way didn't sound right. "That's not—"

"Excellent." Herb rubbed his thin hands together. "I can use that." He pointed at me. "Just you make sure Chelsea knows I get my turn with him too."

"Sure." *Wait. What?*

He turned and strode from the room. I shook my head. At least he hadn't followed up about his curation class. And whatever Herb had in mind, it couldn't scar Jordan too much.

I shifted in my chair. Could it?

The phone rang on my desk, and I snatched it up. "San Benedetto Paranormal History Museum. This is Maddie."

"Hi, this is Ronald from the inspection department."

Augh. My shoulders tightened. "Hi. How's it going?"

"Good. I mean... You know."

I knew. "Sorry. It was a dumb question. What can I do for you?"

"I just called to tell you that the inspection's been finalized. You're good to go."

I sagged against my chair. "We're... You mean we're done?"

"Yep. You can go ahead with your Halloween opening as planned."

"That's..." *Amazing. A relief. About time.* "Thank you. What about you?"

"Me?"

"What's happening with the department now that Ira's... Will there be a memorial service?"

"We'll do something small at Town Hall." He paused. "His ex left town yesterday, I heard."

"Ah." I wasn't surprised she hadn't stuck around. She hadn't seemed the grieving-widow type. "I'd like to attend the memorial, if that's okay."

"I'm sure it will be. I'll make sure you get the information."

I steeled myself. *May as well be direct.* "Who's taking Ira's job?"

"Uh... I am. I'm the new chief inspector as of yesterday."

My scalp prickled. "Congratulations. And thanks for calling me personally."

"It was the least we could do after... everything. I'll send you that info about the memorial."

"Thanks."

He disconnected. I drummed my fingers on the desk.

So Ronald had gotten the job. But was it motive for murder? Under ordinary circumstances, I'd think not. But if there was corruption in the department, the guy in charge would be better placed to cover it up.

Assuming Ronald was involved. And that was a big assumption.

Standing, I grabbed my cell phone off the desk and jammed it in the rear pocket of my jeans. I needed to get out of here before—

"Can I vent?" Leo walked into the room and dropped into one of the chairs in front of my desk.

I sighed and leaned one hip against the desk. "Sure. What's up?"

"Am I still a part of the museum?" he asked.

Heaviness weighted my stomach. "What do you mean? Of course you are. You're working on our enhanced reality app."

"Yeah, and it's coming along. But then what? Herb is curating. Chelsea is doing her thing preserving the artifacts. Am I just taking tickets?"

I swallowed. I'd known this was coming. And I'd been avoiding it, because I hadn't been sure how to handle the discussion. "You've always been a little overqualified for a paranormal museum."

"So that's it. I *am* going to be the ticket taker."

"You're graduating next spring. How would you *like* to use your degree?"

He studied his black motorcycle boots. "I want to code things, make things."

"Like our app. But... Not a lot of coding happens at the museum. I guess... I guess I hoped the app would be a good way for you to show off your chops to a potential employer."

"You're saying you don't need me."

A dull ache pierced my chest. "I'm saying we both know you've outgrown the museum. And if you want to stay and take tickets..." I swallowed. "I'll fire you." And I would.

There was nothing wrong with mundane work like taking tickets and packing boxes. I did plenty of it. But I did it building something for myself. And Leo would be wasting the computer skills he'd spent so much time and money learning if he stayed.

"Got it." He rose and strode from my office.

"Leo, that's not—" Grimacing, I let my hand drop to my side. *Not what I meant.* But I'd screwed that up too.

chapter twenty-three

TELEPATHIC SPIRIT COMMUNICATOR

United States, 1910

This dial-type planchette was developed by Spiritualist W.T. Braham in 1910. It consists of a 17" rectangular cardboard base with an alphanumeric strip along the top. Beneath is the planchette, which runs along a track beneath the letters and numbers.

During the séance, the medium rested his fingers on the ends of the planchette to receive messages from the spirits.

When you think your day can't get any worse, it's a good sign that it's about to do just that. I strode into the museum's foyer. The glass door closed slowly behind Leo and swept open again. I had to take a quick step back to avoid getting knocked down.

Mason reared away, his blue eyes widening. "Whoa. Sorry. Where's Jordan?"

"Ah…" I looked around the foyer as if Jordan might sprout like a carnation from its linoleum floor. "He's been working with Chelsea. Let's go find them."

He nodded. "Thanks."

I strode past the ticket booth and toward the offices. "Is everything okay?"

Mason clawed a hand through his mane of blond hair. "Yeah. I mean, I don't know."

I paused beside the wheelchair elevator and rocked slightly on my feet. "You don't know?"

"Jordan's been acting secretive lately," he said in a low voice. "I want to think it's just the usual teen stuff. But things have been tense with his mother."

My shoulders tightened. "Oh. I'm sorry to hear that," I said in a neutral tone.

I'd broken up with Mason because I hadn't wanted to be a home wrecker. Not that he and Belle had been together when we'd gotten started, but family was important. Jordan was important. I'd been careful to give them space, because if Jordan had a shot at an intact family, he deserved it. But now that was off the table.

And this isn't your fault. You're not responsible for Belle's actions. Stay out of it.

"She wants custody of Jordan. Full custody."

"What?" Pressure heated the top of my skull. "How can she—?" I bit off the words. I hadn't stepped between Mason and Belle when they'd started seeing each other again. I wasn't going to do it now. "Sorry. I'm just surprised after everything that happened."

"According to the law, nothing happened," he said bitterly. "The only thing stopping her from taking Jordan is Jordan. He says he wants to keep living with me. But I think he's mainly saying that to spite his mother."

"And spite is something you can't encourage." My chest compressed. Belle wasn't the most stable parent, and I was on Team Mason. But if Jordan was just staying with Mason to stick it to his mom, that wasn't a firm foundation for a family unit. "What a mess," I muttered.

"Yeah. The thing is, I'm afraid if she even gets partial custody, she'll take off and I'll never see either of them again."

My heart sank. That wasn't... totally unrealistic. And there was nothing I could do. I nodded. "Let's get Jordan."

Chelsea's office door was ajar. I knocked on it then walked inside. Chelsea glanced up from her desk. The only thing on it was the notebook she'd been writing in.

Jordan sat at a small round table in the corner. He flipped through a three-ring binder of white and mustard-colored pages.

"Hey," Mason said. "Time's up. You've got homework."

Jordan scowled. "Fine." He shut the binder and stood. "I'll come back tomorrow."

"Tomorrow's Saturday," Mason said. "We're going to the science fair."

Jordan rolled his eyes. "Whatever." He slouched from the office.

Mason shot me an apologetic look and followed.

"How'd it go with Jordan?" I asked Chelsea.

"He's alright," she said. "And I need to buy another dehumidifier."

I sighed. "How much?"

She named a figure, and I flinched. "You sure we need it?" I asked.

Chelsea sat back and folded her arms. "I'm sure."

"Okay," I said. "Write up a purchase order, and I'll get on it." And I fled before I could be hit with any more bills or irate employees.

Fridays were usually ladies' night at the local microbrewery. But Harper had a public meeting of the town council and Adele had been complaining about not enough quality time with Dieter. Ladies' night was off.

So I'd made plans to have dinner with Jason and absolutely *not* ask him about the murders. If he wanted to bring them up though, that was fine by me.

Alas, he did not. We dined at our favorite chop house and talked about everything but his work.

"How's your sister doing with the wedding planning?" Jason speared a piece of steak. His navy tie was flung over one shoulder. He'd come straight from work and was still in his detective's clothes, a navy suit and white shirt.

"Since it's in Sicily, I'm not really involved." And for that at least I was grateful. I sat up straighter in my straight-backed chair. Since he'd brought it up... "About the wedding..."

He looked up, his expression wary. "Yeah?"

Want to be my plus-one? I smoothed the red tablecloth. "Do you want to go to the... ah..."

His brown eyes were serious. The points of his suit jacket collar were smooth and even and perfect. And I was willing to bet there wasn't a blot of oil on the napkin in his lap. He wouldn't have time to disrupt his life for Sicily.

"...go to the harvest festival with me?" I blurted.

"Yes, but what does that have to do with your sister's wedding?"

"Nothing." Tingling heat swept my cheeks. *Stop being such a coward.* It was wrong to assume what was going on in Jason's head. "I was just thinking... Since it's a long flight to Sicily, I'm taking ten days off and my mom and I are going ahead of time."

A waiter strode past carrying two goblets of red wine. At a nearby table, a couple, sitting side-by-side, laughed. The male half of the couple pulled his date closer.

"I still don't see the harvest festival connection," Jason said. "But can you take the time off with the new museum just opening?"

"Yeah. I mean... sure. The wedding's in March. Things should be settled at the museum." But *would* the board think I was shirking my duties? Would the staff?

I shook myself. I was distracting myself again.

"It probably will take a week just to get over the jet lag," he said. "Makes sense to go early."

"Plus, Sicily, right? I've never been there. Have you?"

"No. My ex and I went to Italy on our honeymoon, but we didn't hit Sicily."

My stomach dropped. Jason rarely talked about his ex-wife. I rallied. "Have you ever thought of seeing more of the country?"

He shook his head. "Maybe, some day. But who has the time?" He smiled. "I'm not a Paranormal Museum director."

"Oh." I tried to ignore the disappointment spiraling in my gut. "And that's Paranormal *History* Museum now, buddy. I've stepped up in the world."

He laughed. "Okay. Paranormal history. But why are you asking about Italy?"

"I just thought... I mean, you're welcome if you want to come along..." I smoothed the front of my green knit top. "It would mean a week off work if you wanted to get over the jet lag. You wouldn't have to come for the whole ten days."

Jason's expression grew serious. "Do you want me to come?"

"Of course I'd love it if you came. But I understand if you can't," I said quickly. "It's no big deal."

"I'm not sure I have the vacation time."

Right. "I understand. It's not an easy thing. You can't just drop everything and run to Sicily at the drop of a hat. Really, it's fine."

"You keep saying *it's fine*," he said, "but is it?"

I laid my hand atop his and smiled. I'd suspected he couldn't do it, and he couldn't. It was nothing personal. But disappointment tightened my chest.

"Of course it is," I said. "Besides, weddings are boring. Why eat up precious vacation time on one? So tell me about the investigation." *Oh, damn.* Why did I say that?

His hand pulled slightly away. "There's not much I can say. It's ongoing. Is there anything you want to tell me?"

"Nothing I already haven't." I sipped my Zinfandel. "What about that stolen truck?" I had a right to know about that at least, since it had run me off the road.

"Taken from a gas station," Jason said. "It belonged to a local senior citizen, who left his keys in the ignition when he went to pay for his gas."

So it wouldn't have taken a master thief to steal it. Not that that narrowed the list of suspects. "Oh."

"We found it abandoned by the lake. We dusted it for prints but haven't found anything. There were no video cameras aimed its way when it was stolen. Right now, we don't have much."

I rallied. "At least the owner got it back."

"Slightly dented. The driver was a fool to tangle with that tank of yours."

"My truck's sturdy, even if the mileage isn't great." And now we were making small talk. I set down my glass. "I'm sorry. I feel off tonight, and I'm saying all the wrong things. I told myself I wasn't going to ask about your investigation, and I did it anyway. I shouldn't have. I know you can't discuss it."

"Why do you feel off?"

"Getting the new museum started, my sister's wedding... Pick one."

"Ah. The wedding." Jason's careful expression returned.

I angled my head. "No, it's *not* making me think about my own marital status, or lack thereof. But I knew you'd think that, so I've been freaking myself out about asking you if you wanted to be my plus-one."

"Do you *want* to move our relationship to the next level?"

"No, I'm happy with the way things are." A nice, adult relationship. One where I could admit when I was feeling uncertain. Emotional maturity. Strong communication. They were the foundations of a solid couple.

So why did it all feel so wrong?

chapter twenty-four

AURAGRAPH BY HAROLD SHARP

England, 1946

This circular ink sketch is an automatic drawing of a person's aura by Harold Sharp (1890 – 1980) and his spirit guide, Chin Shih. Typically, Sharp would draw the colors first and superimpose the ink drawing over them.

Sharp's connection to the spirits began in childhood. He regularly saw the spirit of a monk, who he later determined was one of his spirit guides. His interest in spiritualism was piqued in the 1920s, after he visited Arthur Conan Doyle's psychic museum and bookshop in Westminster.

Since the museum had been closed for reopening (ha), I'd been enjoying my weekends off. But I couldn't take time off from GD. So Saturday morning I drove to the new museum and fed the cat.

Beside my desk, I crouched next to him as he crunched kibble. His lean shoulders hunched. Had the ebony cat lost some weight since we'd switched museums? I hoped that was only because he had more room to explore and wasn't a stress reaction to the move.

The glass door to the museum banged shut. I stiffened. The museum staff had the weekend off, and I wasn't expecting workmen today.

I straightened to standing, my knees cracking, and I winced at the sound. Why had I left the door unlocked? Stealthily, I tiptoed to my office door and peered out.

Jordan, wearing a backpack, jeans, and a t-shirt, vanished down the stairs into the museum proper.

I waited a moment, then I followed. Jordan was supposed to be at a science fair with his dad. Maybe his appearance here was innocent, but maybe it wasn't.

I padded through the aisles. The museum had been designed like a unicursal labyrinth. There was only one way in and one way out (emergency exits not included). I wasn't worried about losing the teen.

I walked past the haunted bowling lane. I wandered past the Zoltan fortune telling machine. I crept past antiques from the spiritualist era, through the British magic room, and around our international exhibits.

I rounded a narrow corner. The blond boy stood with his back to me, a framed photo in his hands. I glanced at the empty spot on the wall. Paul Foster Case was missing. I cleared my throat.

Jordan whirled, gripping Case's frame. It's black backing lay on the floor by his track shoes.

I arched a brow. "Aren't you supposed to be at a science fair?"

His freckled face reddened. "We don't have to leave for another thirty minutes."

I checked the clock on my phone. Since Jordan wasn't old enough to drive, it would take him nearly that to get home. "You're cutting it close, aren't you? What are you doing here?"

"I found a better frame." He set down the photo and unzipped his backpack, withdrawing an elaborate, black-painted frame.

My mouth pursed. "Where'd you find that?"

"I used it last Halloween for a haunted photo—you know, one with eyes that glow? I found it in a thrift store. I got a little paint on your old frame. When I tried to get it off, I chipped off some of the original paint. I thought this would make up for it." He handed the new frame to me.

I studied it gravely and tried not to wonder what he'd been doing with paint in the museum. The frame was a little overblown for Paul Foster Case's severe aesthetic, but it would draw more attention to the photo.

I nodded. "I like it. You're sure your Dad won't mind you taking it?"

"It's my frame," Jordan said, his voice rising. "I bought it."

"Okay. Then thanks."

His shoulders relaxed. "Do you want to...?" He nodded to the picture on the floor.

"No, no. You can swap out the photo."

Carefully, he removed the photo of Case and set it in the new frame. Jordan replaced the backing and hung it on the wall. Hands on his slim hips, he stepped away to study it, then reached out and straightened the frame. "I wish..."

"What?"

He sighed. "I think you're right. There is something more magic about not knowing, about having to wait for the secret society letter in the mail."

"Yeah. But by mail, internet, or in person, the occult can be dangerous."

"How?"

"Because..." My brain stumbled for the right words. "I think there *is* magic in this world. But when people take it too seriously, when they start taking themselves too seriously, they lose themselves and separate from what matters. They become vulnerable to bad people, to lies, and they can't connect with the real magic."

"What's the real magic?"

There was something a different famous occultist had once said... *Infinite worlds.* "That each person is a world in themselves. We all have inner lives. And though no one else can completely know another, we can explore parts of those other lives through love."

My face warmed. And what was I doing getting philosophical with a not-quite teenager? What did I know of Jason's inner world? What did he know of mine? I was afraid the answer was *not much.* And what did that say about us? About me? Had I been so self-involved that I just hadn't... bothered?

"Sorry." I cleared my throat. "Hanging out with all this history can put me in a metaphysical frame of mind."

"No, no," he said, his fair brow puckering. "I get it. I think. Or I *had* it. And now it's gone. But for a second, I felt..." He studied the laminate floor. "It's gone now."

I smiled. "That's a lot like the paranormal. The experience is there, then it's gone. You can't prove anything and are left wondering if you imagined it all. And you're going to be late for that science fair. Let me give you a ride home."

I drove Jordan home.

He sat silently and stared out the passenger window. We did not have a heart-to-heart about his mother. We didn't say much to each other at all. But I was a boring adult, and he was entitled to his own private inner world too.

I thought about my own behavior the last few days. I'd lost touch with what was important, what mattered.

People mattered. Not just the people close to me—though they were the ones it was easiest to love. But my community mattered.

And even though I hadn't known Ira or Frank well, their deaths were connected to my museum somehow. And their lives had mattered. My chest constricted. Their worlds had mattered.

I parked in the brick alley behind the old museum, and we climbed the concrete stairs. Jordan unlocked the studded metal door.

Mason jerked it open, scowling. "Where have you—?" His head rocked backward. "Oh. Maddie. Hi."

"Jordan finished up some work at the museum," I said. "I think he's worked off his crime."

Jordan blinked. "Wait. You mean, I'm done?"

I met his father's blue-eyed gaze. I gave him an up-to-you smile.

Mason nodded. "If she says you're done, you're done."

"But... I don't mind," Jordan said. "I mean, I can keep going."

"I don't know what else to put you to work doing," I said.

"What about tickets?" Jordan asked. "When the museum opens, I mean."

"You're going to be in school," I said.

"But not all day," he reasoned. "What about weekends?"

"Maybe when you get a little older," Mason said. "Then you can apply at the museum."

The pre-teen grunted. He slouched past Mason into the apartment.

I raised my hands in a defensive gesture. "I didn't encourage it."

Mason barked a laugh. "Are you kidding? It's a paranormal museum. You didn't have to encourage it." He glanced over his shoulder. "Thanks," he said more quietly. "I know he was more work than help. But I needed for him to feel the consequences of his actions. I'll make this up to you."

"It was fine. And you're welcome." I hesitated on his doorstep.

"Want to come to the fair?" he asked. "Jordan built an electric motor."

I raised a brow. "*Jordan* did?"

Mason smiled. "I may have given him some advice, but he did all the work." He sobered and dropped his voice. "I invited Belle to the fair, but... She can't make it."

A lump hardened my throat. *Belle.* If she wanted full custody, this wasn't the way to show it. I forced a smile. "Sure. Why not?"

chapter twenty-five

Collection of Athames Used *in Magical Rituals*

United States, circa 1960

Athames are used in several magical traditions, including Wicca, pagan-ism and neo-paganism. The use of a knife to focus one's intention during spellcasting dates back at least to the Renaissance.

Science fairs aren't what they used to be. I didn't see a single dinosaur diorama, solar-system mobile, or volcano gushing red-tinted corn syrup.

But an entire section of the school gym was devoted to robotics. Computer screens displaying fractals and sound waves and other weird designs lined the rectangular tables.

Jordan's project was already up, having been put on display the night before. The teen flipped a switch, and the motor whirred quietly. "It's electric," he said. "I used magnets."

"Cool," I said. "How?"

"The magnets interact," he said. "They alternate between attracting and repelling each other, and that makes the motor spin."

I nodded slowly. "Okay. I get it. Sort of." In a vague, science-y way. I believed the science worked. I believed Jordan understood it. But I didn't.

Mason clapped his son's shoulder. "Nice work."

Jordan grunted. His narrow face reddened. "Flying stuff is outside." He turned and slouched toward a set of open exit doors.

Mason drew a deep breath, his chest swelling and relaxing. "I'll have a talk with him tonight about gratitude."

"Kids are tough at that age," I said, sympathetic. "Everything's embarrassing, especially parents."

Mason folded his arms over his black tee, his biceps expanding. "Am I a bad person because a part of me's glad Belle's not here? She *should* be here. But Jordan's been so..." He shook his head. "I don't know how he would have reacted."

"As a wise man once told me, you can't fix everything. Let's go check out the flying stuff."

We walked through two open doors to basketball courts enclosed by high, chain-link fences. Elaborate balloons shaped like zeppelins and steampunk airships floated above the courts.

"Are you going to the Harvest Festival?" I asked.

He nodded. "Sunday night. I'm taking Jordan."

"Maybe I'll see you there."

"Are you going with Jason?"

"We—"

Jordan appeared at his father's side. "Can I get a cupcake?" He jerked his thumb toward a long table beside the gym's tan stucco side.

"Sure." Mason pulled his wallet from the rear pocket of his jeans, opened it, and handed Jordan a fiver.

Jordan hurried off.

I eyed Mason.

He sighed. "It's a little early for cupcakes," he said, "isn't it?"

"Sorry. Was that a judgey look? Because I'm really not. Judging, that is. I mean, it's not like you're feeding them to him daily."

"Want a cupcake?"

"Please. I'm an adult. I can eat garbage whenever I want. So, yes."

We ambled to the table. The caterer, Alex, handed Jordan a cupcake piled with chocolate icing.

"Oh," I said. "Hi."

Alex blinked. "Maddie?"

"The science fair caters?" I asked. Things really *had* changed since I'd been in school. "I'd have thought the band would be here having a bake sale."

"They sort of are," he said. "I'm doing this pro bono. One of the parents financed my ingredients. All the proceeds go to the band."

And Alex got publicity, goodwill, and connections. It was nice to see someone who understood the importance of community.

"Oh, hey," I said. "We've passed our final inspection. The grand opening is happening on Halloween as planned."

He smiled. "That's great news. Congratulations. I'll be ready with mummy fingers and eyeball drinks."

I laughed. "Perfect."

"What kind of cupcake do you want?" Mason asked me and opened his wallet.

"Chocolate. Duh. You don't know me at all, do you?"

Mason grinned. "You'll forever remain a mystery."

I craned my neck, tracking a striped red and yellow hot air balloon. Canned heat dangled from strings beneath. "Huh. I read a book once about some kid scientists who started a UFO scare with balloons like that. The canned heat gave the balloons buoyancy and created an eerie light. I always wanted to try that."

Mason chuckled and handed Alex a bill. "Of course you did. What stopped you?"

"I was afraid I'd set a vineyard on fire," I said. "How are they keeping the balloons from escaping?"

"Robotics." Jordan bit into his cupcake, smearing his mouth with chocolate. "It's really cool." He launched into a detailed explanation. It flew over my head like a science-fair balloon.

Mason stiffened.

"There you are," a woman exclaimed from behind me. "Why aren't you at your motor?"

Jordan's mother, Belle, strode toward us. Though she was a few years younger than me, lines crinkled the corners of her eyes. Her longish auburn hair was done up in a loose bun. Over her t-shirt and jeans, she wore a denim blazer. A pink rose was embroidered over the heart.

Jordan finished his cupcake. "Oh. Hi, Mom."

Belle stopped short, her smile fading. "You're *not* eating a cupcake at this hour?" she said loudly.

Jordan belched. "Not anymore."

Belle whirled on Mason. "Seriously? What were you thinking? You know how he reacts to sugar. And why isn't he at his table? He's supposed to be demonstrating his motor to the judges."

"The judging happened last night," Mason said.

Belle sucked in a breath. "Oh, so it's my fault I wasn't here?"

Mason shook his head. "I didn't say that."

"You're saying I'm a bad mother?" she demanded.

My stomach writhed. Then, since it has no sense of propriety, it growled. A few parents glanced over their shoulders at us.

"And what's *she* doing here?" Roughly, Belle motioned toward me.

"Getting a cupcake." I plucked one from the table and nodded to Mason. "Thanks." I strode into the gym.

My flight wasn't *complete* cowardice. I had the feeling that me hanging around would only make things worse.

I studied a water tank with wood cylinders and a wood disk floating in it. The placard beside it read: *Buoyancy of Floating Cylinders.* "I don't get it."

I bit into the cupcake. Hot damn, there was sour cream frosting inside. *Genius.* I'd have to talk to Alex about adding these to our grand opening menu.

Jordan came to stand beside me. "The disk floats with its circular cross section face up. The cylinder floats with its circular cross section partially submerged in the water. The experiment measures how the tilt angle depends on the aspect ratio."

"Uh, huh." I nodded wisely. "Aspect ratios. Right."

"It belongs to a friend of mine," he explained.

"Gotcha." I took another bite of the cupcake. We studied the bobbing wood.

"Sorry about my mom," he said.

My heart pinched. "There's nothing to be sorry for." He wasn't responsible for his parents. "You have two parents who love you. That's what matters." But the platitude rang hollow.

One of the gym doors clanged shut, and I glanced toward the sound. Wiping her eyes, Belle stormed through the exhibits. Parents with startled expressions watched her path. Without a backward glance, she strode through the doors to the parking lot.

I realized Jordan had edged behind me. Had he been hiding?

The boy cleared his throat. "You know, a friend of mine has a project in the robotics section. Want to see it?"

Mason walked into the gym and looked around. He caught my eye and strode toward us.

"Let's see what your father wants to do," I said.

Mason gripped his son's shoulder. "What next?"

"Robotics?" I asked brightly.

"Nah." Jordan folded his arms, his chin jutting forward. "It's okay. I've seen it all."

"Maddie hasn't seen it all," Mason gently reminded him.

"Whatever you two want to do is fine with me," I said. "I'm still blown away by the airships..." I trailed off. *The airships.*

I glanced toward the twin doors to the basketball courts. A gray-haired man bent, wedging one open again. Belle must have knocked it closed when she'd stormed out.

The airships. The mummy. I stilled, my heart thumping. Was the solution that obvious?

chapter twenty-six

CURSED COWBELLS

Sweden, 1982

These bells are reputed to bring death to those who heard their ringing. The bells were donated to San Benedetto by their sister city in Sweden. The gift celebrated the start of San Benedetto's Christmas Cow tradition. Soon after receiving the bells, every member of San Benedetto's Christmas Cow committee died.

The bells are considered so dangerous, they are bound in a protective binding box dating back to 17th century Germany. The box has been magically consecrated. The symbols you see on its glass and sides are protective wards, designed to keep the curse from injuring anyone else.

Suspicion is a terrible thing. It's even worse without proof one's suspicion is correct. So I went back to the beginning—or at least, back to the beginning for me.

Ladies Aid.

I stood with my mother in their Grand Hall. Devoid of exhibits or rows of chairs, it was as cavernous as the school gym, our voices echoing off the wood floor and walls.

"I don't know what you expect to find." My mother tugged lightly on her squash blossom earring then straightened her head. "The man wasn't killed here."

"But he was put here."

She brushed an invisible piece of lint from the sleeve of her periwinkle blazer. "In *your* sarcophagus."

So help me, I was more pleased that she'd correctly identified it as a sarcophagus than annoyed by the implied blame. I walked to the door to the rear parking lot and tugged on the latch.

"We fixed the lock," my mother said.

I pushed open the door and stared into the rear lot. It was empty. The Saturday afternoon sun was already low, the phantom of winter creeping closer. I studied the rear of the bank building on the other side of the lot.

"The police already combed the area for clues," my mother said. "I doubt you'll find anything there."

I blew out my breath, stepped back inside, and let the door swing shut. It closed heavily. I jiggled the latch. They really *had* fixed the lock.

"See?" my mother said.

Eliza strode into the Grand Hall. "What's going on?" Her hatchet nose twitched.

"Maddie's attempting to recreate the crime."

"Why?" Eliza scowled.

Cora wafted into the room in a billowy haze of purple caftan. "Recreate the crime? What a wonderful idea. Shall I be the body?" She walked to the middle of the hall, clapped her arms to her sides, and stiffened.

"That's not..." *helpful.* But it was, sort of. "The body was frozen, stiff," I said slowly. "That would have made it more difficult to sneak it inside. I mean, it couldn't have been curled up and then unbent to put in the sarcophagus, could it?"

"Have *you* ever tried unfolding a frozen piece of meat?" Eliza said.

"Really, Eliza," my mother reproved.

"What?" Eliza bristled. "That's all the poor man was at that point. *He was gone.*"

"She's right," Cora said out of the corner of her mouth, keeping the rest of her body still. "His spirit had moved on months ago. The corpse was only a shell."

My mother sighed. "You're both right, of course. It just seems disrespectful."

"Killing him, wrapping him up like a mummy, and stuffing him in that fancy coffin was even more disrespectful," Eliza pointed out.

"Sarcophagus," my mother corrected.

"Whatever," Eliza said.

"Mm," I said, trying to get everyone back on track. "Bringing the body through this door Friday after everyone had left seems the most obvious delivery method. That assumes the killer knew about the broken lock though." But was there another way?

"Lots of people knew about that door." Eliza glowered at my mother. "I told you and *told* you we should have had it repaired. But no—"

"Who knew?" I asked. "Exactly?"

"All our members," Eliza said promptly.

"What about the building inspectors?" I asked.

"It was hardly a matter for the inspection department," my mother said.

"But they could have known," Eliza said. "They all have relatives in Ladies Aid."

"Nonsense," my mother said. "None of our members would have told an outsider about that door. Ladies Aid secrets stay within Ladies Aid."

"Your daughter knows about it," Eliza said pointedly.

"Only after a body was discovered in her sarcophagus," my mother said, indignant. "No one outside Ladies Aid knew about that broken lock."

"Fran's right," Cora mumbled through her clenched teeth. "What happens in Ladies Aid, stays in Ladies Aid."

"Silence is golden," my mother agreed.

Eliza's brown eyes narrowed to slits.

"What about the caterer, Alex?" I asked hastily.

"Probably," my mother said. "He was here Friday. All sorts of people were going in and out of that door. *Museum* people were going in and out."

"But the door was propped open so people could bring the exhibits inside," I said. "It wasn't being opened and closed. Like you said, I had no idea the lock was broken until after the body was discovered."

"That's true," my mother admitted.

"Who propped it open?" I asked.

"I did," Eliza said. "I used a door stopper, and it stayed open until everyone left. Then I closed it."

"Hm." I wandered toward the kitchen. Cora unfroze, and the three women trailed behind me.

I sniffed. The kitchen still smelled of smoke though the walls and ceiling had been scrubbed clean of soot. "I can still smell that fire."

"Oh, that's not from the fire," my mother said. "That's from Marybelle forgetting a pot on the stove yesterday. She burned out its bottom."

"It's not the first time she's done that." Eliza's gray eyebrows drew downward. "She did it that Friday too, remember? We worried the smell would spread to the Grand Hall for your soft opening. When I'm back in charge, only authorized personnel will have access to the kitchen."

"It was a good thing that caterer arrived when he did," my mother said. "He got to it before the smoke got too bad."

"Such a nice man," Cora said. "He helped us air out the kitchen."

"Which he refused to use afterward," Eliza said tartly.

"He does have his own professional kitchen," my mother said. "There was no sense in him coming here to cook for the night."

"He helped air the kitchen out?" I asked. "How?"

"He opened the window." My mother angled her head toward the window I'd used.

"That window was unlocked," I said slowly. "Who closed the window that night?"

"I couldn't say," my mother said.

Eliza glared. "You *should* be able to say."

"The point," Cora said, "is that it was closed. Not who closed it."

"The point is that it was unlocked," Eliza snapped.

"Which hardly matters since the lock on the Grand Hall door was broken," my mother said.

"It's lackadaisical." Eliza braced her fists on her broad hips. "Like the rest of you two's leadership."

"That's hardly fair," Cora said. "Fran is horribly organized."

My mother's brow pinched. "Horribly?"

"You know what I mean," Cora said. "We all love your organization skills."

Eliza snorted. "Ha."

"What do you mean, *ha?*" my mother asked. "What's *ha?*"

I cleared my throat. "It's possible that—"

"I mean things are going to change around here after tomorrow." Eliza stuck out her chin.

The election was tomorrow? *Eeesh.* "You know," I said, "I'm just going to—"

"Oh, Eliza," Cora said. "Can't we just get along?"

"No," Eliza and my mother snarled.

"Go," I finished, and hurried out. What happened in Ladies Aid could and should stay in Ladies Aid. And I didn't need to know.

The idea of cooking dinner did not fill me with enthusiasm. So I drove to the Sunshine Cafe.

When I walked in, the owner was standing on a stepladder. He taped paper Halloween decorations to a front window.

I nodded to him, glanced at the *Please Seat Yourself* sign, and looked around. Wynnona sat by herself at a table. Her head was bent, her curling brown hair falling toward a plastic menu.

I hesitated, then walked to her table. "Hi."

The caterer's wife looked up. Twin lines formed between her eyebrows. "Maddie, from the museum, right?"

"Right. Can I join you?"

She leaned back in her chair and motioned to the empty chair opposite. "Sure."

I pulled it out and sat. A waitress bustled to our table. Wynnona ordered a chef's salad. I ordered a cheeseburger to go. The waitress strode into the kitchen.

"Do the police have any idea who put Ira in your coffin?" She cradled the coffee mug resting on the table in both hands.

Sarcophagus. And I really needed to let the semantics go. "If they do," I said levelly, "they haven't told me. How are you holding up?"

"Me?" Her shoulders hunched. "Fine. Why wouldn't I be?"

I exhaled. "You and Ira were close."

She looked up. Her gaze sharpened. "I told you we were friends."

"Yeah." Wincing, I shoved my hands in the pockets of my museum hoodie. "There was some talk about your friendship at Town Hall."

Wynnona hissed an inward breath and set her mug down hard. The brown liquid inside tidal waved but didn't breach the sides. "Janice. What did she say?"

I didn't respond, and her face colored. She looked toward the paper bats swaying in the window.

"People make fun of men's mid-life crises," she said. "The sports cars, the younger women. They don't talk about what women go through. We get older too. Our bodies and looks change. And suddenly we're not worth as much anymore. Of course everyone denies that." She turned the mug on the table. "I didn't think my sense of self was wrapped up in my looks or my body. The change hurt more than I expected."

"What happened?" I asked in a low voice.

"I fell in love." She exhaled a rusty laugh. "Or I thought I did. Ira paid attention to me in a way I'd forgotten about. And it touched something inside me. I was a girl again, in the throes of a teen crush. And I had the emotional maturity level to match." She sipped her coffee, set it down, and met my gaze. "I screwed up. I nearly ruined my marriage. I *would* have ruined it if Alex had found out."

"You had an affair?"

She nodded and swallowed. "But our romance didn't give me any insight into who might have killed Ira," she said hurriedly. "I broke it off about a month before he disappeared. The police don't need to know, do they? I just... I know I deserve whatever I get. A mid-life crisis is no excuse. But I don't want to hurt Alex. He's a good man."

"I think," I said, "if you went to the police yourself, it would be easier to keep it quiet—easier than them finding out and coming to your house for an interview." Especially since I'd already told Jason about the rumored affair.

"And the sooner you tell the police," I continued, "the better."

She nodded, her face creased with misery. "You're right, of course. I will."

I hoped she was telling the truth. "Did Ira have any enemies?"

She laughed shakily. "Janice wasn't too happy with him, though I think she hated me more. They'd been seeing each other before..." She swallowed and looked toward the paper bats in the windows.

"What about the other inspectors?"

"Why would they...?" Pursing her lips, she angled her head. "There was some tension between Ira and Ronald. I think Ira felt Ronald was... challenging his authority?"

As leader of their inspection shakedown? Or had Ronald been outside the game and starting to notice something was wrong? "What about with any of the building owners?"

"No one enjoys a building inspection," she said dryly. "But I don't think Ira was worried about anyone. There were no threats, if that's what you mean. At least not while we... None that he mentioned to me."

The waitress appeared at our table with a paper bag. She set it on the table. "You can pay at the register," she told me.

"Thanks," I said.

She nodded and strode away.

I rose and collected my food. "And thanks for telling me about Ira," I said to Wynnona.

If it was true that he usually went for younger women, maybe there'd been more to the affair than lust. Had he loved her?

She smiled faintly. "Just wait until you hit your fifties. You'll understand."

I hoped I never did.

chapter twenty-seven

Spirit Trumpet

Ohio, circa 1853

This cylindrical cone was used to amplify the voices of the dead. This trumpet once belonged to spiritualist medium Jonathan Koons. When Koons channeled the spirits, he'd place his mouth on the narrow mouthpiece. This enabled the spirits' messages to be more clearly heard.

Trumpets became popular tools for mediums and for the general public. By the 1920s, specialty retailers like E.A. Eckel of Indiana were advertising them for two to three dollars, depending on the features included.

To the right, you can see an example of a 1920s Eckel trumpet with a "luminous" band at its end. It was originally sold for $2.50.

Harper slid into the booth. My friend glanced around the microbrewery and shrugged out of her camel blazer. A waiter stared, stumbling. "Where's Adele?" She slid a finger between her olive skin and the collar of her turtleneck.

I pushed a plastic basket of curly fries and a pale ale across the table to her. "Er, I didn't invite her."

Harper's dark brows rose. Waitstaff bustled past the giant copper vats. Voices rose and fell. I was lucky I'd been able to get a table. The Bell and Brew was packed most Saturday nights. I'd arrived early to secure a table.

"Is she busy with Dieter?" She plucked a curly fry from the red plastic basket.

"I didn't ask. I wanted to talk to you about something a little... sensitive."

Harper dropped the fry. Her expression flattened. "And this is a bribe?"

"No, I just ordered too much. The beer's the bribe."

Huffing a laugh, she braced her elbows on the wooden table. "Okay. What's going on?"

There are limited reasons to kill—unless you're insane. And I didn't think our murderer was insane. People kill for gain—for love, for money, for power. They kill for revenge. Or they kill to protect—their egos, their lives, their livelihoods. I didn't think gain was the motive in this case.

"Ira's ex-wife didn't kill him," I said. "She wasn't in California when he was stuck in my sarcophagus. And if he was having a fling with Janice, well, she's not married. Unless you know something I don't, there are no angry husbands or boyfriends in the wings to bump Ira off. That leaves corruption."

Harper stiffened. "You have no evidence there's any corruption."

"And yet," I said carefully, "the chief building inspector's been murdered for no apparent reason. And so has the owner of one of the buildings he was involved in inspecting."

Harper didn't respond, and a weight seemed to press me deeper into the red faux-leather seat. My friend was honest, but she was now part of town government. I guess I should have been used to being iced out by Jason. Somehow it hurt more coming from Harper.

She exhaled slowly and shook her head. "Maddie, there's—"

"Maddie?" Herb appeared beside our booth. "There you are." He slid in next to me, forcing me to scootch over.

"Herb, this isn't—"

"You'll be happy to know the police have returned the sarcophagus," he said.

I blinked. "They have?" I'd been sure they'd keep it for the trial.

The little man preened. "I had a word with a friend. It's all taken care of."

I narrowed my eyes. "How is it—?"

"No, no." He raised a narrow hand. "There's no need to thank me. It's my job. And Leo's augmented reality app is finished."

My heart plunged. He'd finished, and he'd told Herb? Not me? Leo still hadn't returned my calls either. "That's great."

"The app really is amazing," Herb enthused. "Of course, we worked closely together to ensure the pieces are portrayed in a historically coherent and entertaining manner."

Historically coherent? "Of course," I said faintly.

He straightened his striped bow tie. "I'll demonstrate it for you on Monday."

"Great." But I wanted Leo to demonstrate the new app. I wanted things to be okay between us. "Great, great, great."

Herb reached into the inside pocket of his blazer and drew out a card. He slid it across the table to Harper. "Just in case you don't have my contact number."

The phone number was for the museum, and I did *not* roll my eyes. Harper knew the number.

But she studied the card gravely. "Thank you. This will be useful."

He nodded. "It's important the museum and the town maintain open channels of communication."

"Exactly," she said.

"Plus," he said, "I have to get rid of these old cards. Soon they'll be augmented reality."

"What?" I asked. "You didn't tell me that. Is Leo doing that for you?" Why didn't he tell me? *I* wanted an augmented reality business card.

"Of course," he said. "Is there anything else you needed from me?"

"Ah, no," I said. "I can't think of a thing."

Herb stared expectantly, his thick glasses glinting beneath the stained glass lamp.

I sighed. "Herb?"

"Yes?"

"I've been thinking about that curation class. Why don't you go ahead and sign yourself up."

Beaming, Herb pressed his hands to the table and levered himself from the booth. He touched two fingers to an imaginary hat—no doubt a Sam Spade fedora. "I will. Enjoy your night."

Harper eyed me. "I thought you didn't have funds for the curation class."

"I'll figure something out. Besides, his salary's so low, I have to make up for it somehow."

And I *would* boost his salary as soon as we could afford to. And then I remembered I'd need board approval for that too. I shook my head. I'd figure it out. Later.

I sipped my hard cider. I wanted to return to the original topic, skull-duggery at Town Hall, but I couldn't bring myself to do it. The moment had passed.

"Are you going to the harvest festival?" Harper asked.

"Yeah. Jason's taking me. You?"

"Of course." She laughed. "I *have* to go."

We ordered burgers from a passing waiter. Harper and I talked about the museum, the town, her life as a new councilwoman.

Harper sat back in the booth and shoved her plate aside. "I've been thinking."

"Does your head hurt?"

She made a face, and I laughed. "Sorry," I said. "Habit."

"This can't get back to Ladies Aid," she said.

I straightened in my seat. "Why the hell would I tell them anything?"

"They seem to know everything going on anyway," she muttered.

"If you mean my mother, she's currently occupied prepping for tomorrow's snap election. So if you've got something to spill, now's the time." Or was it?

Paranoia crept up my spine and shivered the back of my neck. Two people were dead. If there was some sort of conspiracy... I glanced around the microbrewery.

Dissatisfied with my hasty perusal, I raised myself up in the booth and looked more closely. The booths on either side were packed with people I didn't recognize. I dropped back onto the padded bench. "We're clear," I said more quietly.

She lowered her voice and leaned closer. "An internal investigation of the department was started after Ira's death. I mean, after his body was found."

"I see." I didn't really, but I didn't want to derail her.

"You're not the first person to report rumors of corruption."

I braced my elbows on the table and leaned closer. "Who's investigating?"

"We're starting with a forensic audit," she said.

I sat back in the booth. If inspectors had been taking payoffs, that wouldn't show up in the finances. "Does this audit include an audit of inspected building approvals?"

She nodded. "The question is if policies and procedures were followed or not."

That... might turn something up. But it seemed like a long shot. "I told Jason about the rumors."

"I know." She raised her hands helplessly and dropped them on the table. "Laurel's been spending her free time nosing around Town Hall. I don't think anyone believes there's anything odd about her presence. She *is* investigating Ira's murder. But..."

I met her gaze. "You think it's Mark and Janice."

She sucked in her breath. "What? You can't— No. Why would you think that?"

"Because Ronald just got a promotion, and you'd make sure he didn't if you thought he was up to no good. And if their inspections are being approved when they shouldn't be, odds are someone in permitting is involved too. And Janice and Ira were an item."

"It doesn't make sense," she hissed. "If Ira found out about Janice and Mark... I mean, why would Janice date him?"

"I don't think Ira found out. I think he was in on it. He and Mark were both involved in the inspection for Frostova."

"Then why would Mark or Janice kill him?"

"They wouldn't have," I said, grim. "Not for that at least." If he hadn't been killed to protect someone, that left gain or revenge.

chapter twenty-eight

BOTA Tarot Cards

Los Angeles, 1938

The BOTA Tarot was created by Paul Foster Case, founder of the mail-order mystery school, Builders of the Adytum (BOTA), and artist Jessie Burns Parke. The design of the Major Arcana, court cards, and aces are based on the 1909 Rider-Waite-Smith (RWS) deck. Case changed what he considered "mistakes" on the part of the RWS deck. The cards are black and white as the meditative exercise of coloring the deck was and remains an important part of an initiate's BOTA training.

Because I didn't want to do my Sunday housekeeping, I went to the museum. Also, I had to feed the cat. But when I unlocked the doors, GD didn't come running as he usually did. (Not to greet me, never to greet me—it was all about the food).

Shrugging, I strolled past the ticket booth and toward my office, where I stored the kibble.

A soft sound floated over the top of the warren of exhibits.

I froze, head cocked, listening. The noise came again, a murmur of voices, and I stiffened. Had Jordan and his friends found another way in?

The idea it might be something supernatural didn't bother to cross my mind. I would have *preferred* a ghost, and I wasn't that lucky.

But something about the voices seemed... not exactly cheerful, but not exactly threatening either. I descended the steps into the labyrinth.

Swallowing, I crept through the exhibits, the voices growing alternately closer and farther away. It was a trick of the mazelike structure. Because the top of it was open, sounds that seemed close often weren't.

I hadn't planned it that way. I'd just been too cheap to bring the walls all the way to the ceiling of the old bowling alley. The sound effect now raised the hairs on the back of my neck.

I could distinguish more than one voice in the murmurs, so it definitely wasn't a ghost. Because while I could, possibly, believe in ghosts, I refused to believe a gaggle had descended on the museum for a good gossip.

On tiptoe, I continued through the winding path. I rounded a charcoal corner.

Three strangers, a man and two women, stood facing Herb. They wanded the area with our EMF detectors. GD wound around the ankles of an elegant, platinum blonde.

My curator stood with his back to me in his usual tweed jacket. "And what's the good of a paranormal museum without a haunt of its own?" Herb motioned toward the bowling lane. "According to urban legend, the lane is haunted by three-time winner of the San Benedetto Bowling Tournament, Mike Rotchburns."

The others glanced at each other. The blonde snorted a laugh.

"This was Mike's favorite lane," Herb continued, oblivious.

I coughed lightly, and he jumped. Herb turned, and his eyes widened behind his coke bottle glasses. "Maddie?" He flushed guiltily and motioned in my direction. "This is our director, Madelyn Kosloski. She's the woman responsible for the expansion of our collection."

I blinked. Had I been responsible? The collection had basically dropped into my lap. But if I hadn't helped the donor puzzle out the mystery of his father's death, maybe he wouldn't have thought of the museum when the collection had dropped into *his* lap.

"Hi." I made an awkward wave. "What's going on?"

Herb's gaze shifted to the bowling lane. "A private tour. I thought it would build some good early buzz for the museum."

My eyes narrowed. Private tours usually went on the calendar. And I knew for a fact none had been scheduled for today. "Wonderful." I smiled broadly.

The man, a pudgy fifty-something in spectacles and a dress shirt, hurried forward. He shook my hand. "Remarkable collection. I love what you've done with the artifacts."

"It's such a *relief* to see the paranormal taken seriously," the platinum blonde said. She was well-dressed, in designer jeans and a sweater. The massive diamonds flashing on her fingers looked like they might be real. "It's a nice change from all the haunted-house-style museums."

"Thank you," I said, pleased despite myself. "How do you all know each other?"

"We started as a paranormal investigation group," the man said. "But we discovered a shared interest in supernatural artifacts."

"I started a podcast," the blonde said.

Then this actually *could* be good publicity for the museum. So why had Herb looked like he'd been caught with his hand in the proverbial cookie jar?

"And of course," she continued, beaming, "we all know Herb. I've skunked him out of more than one paranormal acquisition."

The pudgy man laughed. "If you weren't so set on buying everything, you might have the funds for the primo pieces," he told Herb.

Herb's muscles tightened beneath his tweed jacket. "My focus has changed since becoming curator of the museum. Now I'll be looking for pieces that mesh with the existing collection."

A rotund, gray-haired woman sighed. "I'm so jealous. What I wouldn't give for someone to *pay* me to collect. And to work *here*. It's amazing."

"I'll leave you to your tour," I said. "Herb, when you're finished, would you find me in my office?"

"Certainly," he said.

Biting back a smile, I retraced my steps. GD, no doubt remembering who kept the kibble, trotted at my heels.

I refreshed the cat's food and water bowls. Trying to ignore the crunching emerging behind my desk, I sat and studied my calendar.

I'd been right. No private tours had been scheduled for today. Not that Herb couldn't go off-calendar. Neither of us were sticklers for rules. But something smelled. I reviewed my tasks for the coming week and made notes in my paper calendar.

A lined piece of paper with a rough top edge lay on my desk. Frowning, I picked it up. A childish scrawl raced across the white paper.

The Story of Builders of the Adytum!

The Builders of the Adytum is this sort of secret society (but not really, anyone can join) that's about magic, tarot cards, and ANCIENT WISDOM.

Back in 1922, a guy named Paul Foster Case started Builders of the Adytum (or BOTA) in Los Angeles, California. He was really into magic and wanted to share what he'd learned. He was inspired by another group called the Hermetic Order of the Golden Dawn. (That magical duel you told me about was real—I mean, not real, real, but you're right, they thought it was real).

The Builders of the Adytum are all about tarot cards and something called Qabalah. They have this special course called "The Holy Qabalah" where they teach you about tarot symbols, Qabalah secrets, and other esoteric stuff. It includes meditation techniques and rituals. And they even have their own tarot cards that you can color in.

My dad won't let me sign up for their "correspondence course," even though you can learn all their magic stuff from home. But what if the museum made its own secret society? You could make it an email and get people to sign up for it and get news and stuff from the museum.

P.S. This is Jordan.

I smiled. An email secret society was a good idea. It would also take a lot of work. But it was still a good idea.

More importantly, Mason hadn't called to complain. I didn't blame him for saying *no* to Jordan, who was definitely too young for occult secret societies. But it seemed like he'd taken the request to join BOTA in stride.

There was a soft knock at the door. Herb sidled inside. "They've gone."

"So I assumed." I studied him. "Frenemies of yours?"

He tugged on his bow tie. "Rachel's podcast gets thousands of listeners a week. She's one of the top paranormal podcasters in the area. And her content is evergreen."

I raised my brows. When had Herb started using marketing lingo like *evergreen?*

"The others are big influencers," he continued. "Not just online, either."

I raised one hand to stop him. "It's okay. I trust you."

His muscles slackened beneath his sports jacket.

"But you *do* know you have nothing to prove?" I continued. "Not to them or to me. You're curator for a reason. You're the only one I really trust to do what's right for the collection."

"The only one? Not even Chelsea?" he asked suspiciously.

"Chelsea is a professional, and she wants to do her best. But she doesn't have the passion for the paranormal that you do."

His face reddened. "Have I been going too far?"

"The augmented reality business cards were a stroke of genius," I admitted. And I was determined to get some of my own. "But we won't have Leo forever. Just check in next time you've got a brainstorm, okay?"

I drew my fingers across my scalp. We were losing Leo. But it wasn't the loss of his skillsets that made my stomach bottom.

Herb nodded vigorously. "Right-o. Er, I told them I'd take them out to lunch. On my expense account..."

"Make it the Sunshine Cafe," I said, resigned. At least he couldn't run up too big a bill there.

"Great. Thanks." He hurried from my office.

I called Cora, my mother's co-president at Ladies Aid.

"Maddie, what a surprise. What can I do for you?"

"I need to track down Leo." Cora had been a surrogate mother to him. If anyone knew where he was, she would know.

"Ah. You two do need to talk. I told him..." She sighed. "Well, I'm afraid I won't be Mama Cora forever. He's not a boy anymore."

I grimaced. It looked like changes were coming for us all. I hadn't con-sidered how Leo's growing independence would affect Cora. "I suspect you'll always be Mama Cora to him, even if that role changes somewhat."

"He took his bike to the lake."

And by *bike*, she meant motorcycle. "Thanks."

I added more water to GD's bowl. Then I hurried outside, locking the door behind me, and drove to the lake.

It's not a very big lake—more of an oversized pond. But it was a popular cool-off spot in the summer and make-out spot in the evenings. It was also a nice place to relax and watch the mist rise off the water on a fall morning.

I parked beside Leo's small, black motorcycle. One day, he wanted a Harley. I'd caught him more than once staring longingly through Mason's shop window at the custom-built beauties inside.

I climbed a low hill. Leo sat near the top at the other side, his elbow wrapped around his knees.

"Hey." Ignoring the dampness of the dried grass, I sat beside him.

"Hey," he said.

We didn't speak for a long time. A gothic mist hovered above the water's flat, mercury surface. A bird rustled in the nearby brush.

"I don't want you to go," I said. "I want everything to stay the same. I want everything I love in my life to keep on, and for the things that can get better to get better." I caught myself blinking back tears. "But that's selfish. The people in my life aren't inanimate objects for me to enjoy. They're people, with dreams and possibilities and their own adventures in front of them. And I can't afford to pay you what you deserve."

"I know," he said.

"And—what?" My lips parted.

He turned his head. "I know. You're right. I can't stay at the museum. Not because I don't want to. I do want to. But it would be a waste of my degree. I should be earning more money. I shouldn't be playing small, even if it's comfortable."

I swallowed. "Right."

"I'm going freelance."

"Oh. That's... great. Do you—?"

"I've been taking Herb's augmented reality card on interviews." He grinned.

"You've been interviewing?"

"Yeah. Not a lot. But yeah. Everyone wants one—a card, I mean."

"No kidding. I want one. I can't believe you made one for Herb and didn't make one for me."

His grin broadened. "What's it worth to you?"

"Ah..." I was a little afraid to ask what he planned on charging.

He nudged me with his shoulder. "Don't worry. You'll always get the friends and family discount."

"Thanks."

"Thanks for pushing me." He sobered. "I mean it. You've been a good friend. A real friend. I won't forget it."

My throat tightened. "Right back at you." I stared over the lake. A black bird rose from the mist and soared above the gray outlines of trees.

chapter twenty-nine

AUTOMATIC WRITING SAMPLE BY Hélène Smith

Switzerland, 1894

This sample of Martian writing comes from Swiss medium and channeler Hélène Smith (1861-1929). She became famous in 1900 with the publication of the book about her exploits during trances, From India to the Planet Mars. *She became a good friend of the author of the book, a psychology professor, until the book's publication. She was offended by the professor's attempt to rationalize her experiences from a psychological perspective.*

In addition to automatic writing, Smith engaged in automatic painting. Her art inspired the surrealists, who called her the "Muse of Automatic Writing."

It's painful to look at your own behavior and find it wanting. Painful, but illuminating. I hadn't been all-in with my relationship with Jason. I'd been holding myself back—mostly out of fear.

The last time I'd been all-in with someone, I'd gotten hurt. Badly.

But that's the risk you sign up for. Without accepting it, your heart can't truly be open. And I saw now that I'd been the one to suffer for it. That changed tonight.

Right after I told Jason what I'd learned.

I noodled around the museum, keeping my mind off the coming evening with busy tasks. More calls to potential donors. Scheduling social media posts. Plotting future exhibits. We now had an amazing collection of twentieth-century supernatural art. I wanted to give it its due.

GD watched me for a time, his green eyes glowing. Growing bored, the cat vanished with a flick of his black tail into the warren of exhibits.

At five on the dot, I hurried home to get ready for my date with Jason. I eyed a black cocktail dress and discarded it. We were going to a harvest festival. Sequins would be overkill. I settled for a navy knit top with a plunging neckline that hugged my curves. My boot-cut jeans did the same.

As I slipped dangly silver earrings into my ears, I caught myself rehearsing what I was going to say. *I haven't been all-in on the relationship, and I think you've felt it. But that's on me, not you. And I want to change that. We've gotten comfortable. I'd like to move forward.*

Insides butterflying, I shook my head, setting the earrings swinging. Rehearsing might make me feel better, but it would just end up sounding inauthentic.

I'd just tell him what I felt. I should have told him long ago. *Move forward.*

There was a knock at the front door. I hurried into the living area. Though we were going out, I'd given it a good cleaning. I'd stacked the magazines neatly on the coffee table. I'd arranged the throw blanket over the back of the pale blue couch. I'd dusted the nautical instruments on the bookshelf.

I haven't been all-in on the relationship. But that's on me. We've gotten comfortable. I'd like to move forward.

Stop rehearsing!

I opened the door, and a chill breeze flowed into the room. I smiled at Jason, handsome in a long, gray coat. "Hi. Right on time." I stepped forward and kissed his cheek.

He pressed his hand to my lower back, then stepped away. "Can I come in?"

"Of course. I'm almost ready. I've just got to grab my jacket."

I strode to a small closet and opened the door. Lightly, I bit my bottom lip. This wasn't the time to blast him with a relationship analysis, not after he'd just walked in the door.

Murder first. Romance second. I was fairly certain my caterer was a killer, and he needed to be dealt with before he hurt anyone else.

Jason shut the door behind him.

Pea coat in hand, I turned to face him. "There's something—" we said at the same time.

I laughed self-consciously.

"You go," he said.

"No," I said. "You." Alex could wait another minute.

"Yeah." He ran his hand over his curling dark hair. "I'm not sure how to say this."

"Just say it."

His gaze met mine. "I think we should break up."

He wanted to...? My hands slackened. I caught my coat before it could hit the floor. "Oh."

Jason's long coat hung in perfect folds from his muscular frame. His broad hands were loose, at ease, at his side. The yellow stripes on his tie were a cheerful flash against his dark suit.

I should have known something was wrong when he'd walked in. No one wears a tie to a harvest festival. On the high shelf behind him, my grandfather's sextant gleamed dully. I still hadn't dusted that shelf.

We *couldn't* break up. I'd figured out what was wrong. I just hadn't been trying hard enough. We could fix this. "Jas—"

"You're an amazing woman," he said. "You've made my life so much better. Before we met, I took myself too seriously. I took life too seriously. You changed that. But... Are you in love with me?"

Of course I was... I gripped the coat to my stomach. It pitched sickeningly.

Was I in love with him? I swallowed. "I... haven't been all-in on the relationship, and I guess you felt it. But that's on me, not you."

"It's not on anyone," he said gently. "Sometimes, a relationship just isn't right. It's not you. It's not me. It's the two of us together, and I think I've been holding you back."

"We've gotten comfortable," I whispered.

"And comfort's nice. But I think we both want more."

"Move forward," I said, having a hard time breathing.

"You've got a lot to move forward to," he said. "We both do. We just need to let each other go."

I stared, numb. "Yes," I managed, throat tight. "I think you're right."

"Yeah." Jason looked down at his polished shoes. He nodded. "I'll see you around, Maddie." He turned, opened the door, and walked out.

The door closed behind him. His footsteps retreated down the wooden stairs.

Blinking rapidly, I leaned against the closet door. The coat dropped to the floor. Hurt and rejection whirled through me. I wanted to chase after him.

We could fix this. I'd figured it out. I gasped, forcing air through my lungs.

But of course, I didn't run after him. And it wasn't just pride that held me in place. Deep down, I knew he was right.

Maybe I *had* screwed up by not loving him more fully sooner. But I hadn't. I couldn't force it. Wanting to hold onto him was just me being perverse.

I'd held myself back in the relationship, because deep down, I'd known we weren't right together. He was a good man, and I cared about him. But sometimes, that wasn't enough.

My eyes burned. If I was going to move on, I had to let him go too.

Just... not tonight. A sob caught in my throat.

I cried for a bit. Then I splashed my face with water, freshened my makeup, changed into a Paranormal Museum tee. I drove on autopilot to the harvest festival.

I wasn't feeling it. I wasn't feeling anything but hurt. But the museum was one of the sponsors. And sometimes, when you're feeling it the least, that's the most important time to step out.

I parked in the wide dirt lot. As I'd anticipated, it wasn't crowded on this, the last day of the festival. The evening was warm, but I couldn't seem to shake the chill that gripped me. I grabbed the hoodie from the seat beside me and shrugged it on.

Slipping my phone into my hoodie pocket, I wandered to the entrance. A ticket taker checked my ID and stamped my hand. I walked past the sponsors' sign, with the new Paranormal History Museum logo, and into the sprawling festival grounds.

Strings of paper lanterns hung between tall poles erected for that purpose. Tents and marquees glowed with light, and a harvest moon hung above the nearby vineyard. Wine barrels doubled as small tables in front of food and wine booths. Most were unoccupied.

The tasting tent belonging to Adele's family was on the other side of the festival. Someone had posted arrow signs for her vineyard shortcut to their tent. I moved into the vineyard.

Following the signs, I walked in a daze between rows of fading vines. Their gold and purple leaves, their colors deadened by the night, rustled gently as I passed.

A cloud passed in front of the moon, and the vineyard darkened. But the rows were straight and even. I increased my pace, head down, and I tried not to think of Jason.

My neck corded. It was impossible not to think about Jason.

I clenched my jaw. I could call him, figure things out. I pulled out my phone, my thumb hovering over the screen.

No. No. He'd said what he'd had to say, and he'd meant it, and he'd been *right.*

We couldn't go back. This couldn't be fixed. I jammed my phone back into my pocket. And I didn't hear the footsteps behind me.

"Maddie?"

I turned.

Alex struck my chest with his forearm, knocking me backward. Hands still in my pockets, I stumbled over my own heels and fell to the soft earth.

He loomed over me, his fists clenched. "You shouldn't have talked to my wife."

chapter thirty

VAMPIRE HUNTER'S KIT

England, 19th century

This felt-lined wooden box contains everything the 19th century vampire hunter could desire. It contains two crucifixes, a bottle once containing holy water (now evaporated), a wooden stake and mallet, rosary beads, brass candlesticks for nighttime hunting, a leather-bound Bible, two matching pistols, and a brass powder flask. The box can be locked by turning the two decorative brass crosses on the lid.

I scrambled to my feet. He knew I'd talked to Wynnona? What had he done? "Did you kill Wynnona too?" Nausea choked my throat. *Please, no. Please let me not have caused her death.*

The festival lights glowed on the edges of the darkened vineyard. I'd spoken loudly, but I didn't think it had mattered. We were alone.

"No." The caterer's massive fists clenched and unclenched. "Of course I didn't. I *love* her."

My shoulders sagged. She was alive. But how long would Wynnona stay that way? She must have suspected something after our conversation, or it wouldn't have set Alex off.

Now I just had to stay alive too. I swallowed and jammed my hands in my pockets. My fingers slid across the phone's raised buttons, cool and smooth and comforting. "Wynnona was why you killed Ira, wasn't she?"

"He made a fool of me," Alex snarled. "I paid him off—I thought we were partners. And then he slept with my wife? And when I confronted him, he just shrugged, like it didn't matter."

"So you killed him."

"I reacted."

"How convenient that you have that walk-in freezer," I said, stalling. Alex was stronger and faster than me. I had no illusions about outrunning or outfighting him. My only hope was someone coming along, someone seeing us, stopping him.

I tilted my head. My pulse fluttered in my throat. "Or *was* it convenient? You hired people to work events, but you worked alone in the catering kitchen. You panicked that day when Wynnona said she needed something from the freezer. Then you remembered that Ira wasn't there anymore, didn't you? Was that the first close call?"

"No. I had to get rid of that body. When I saw your sarcophagus... I didn't want to just dump it in the lake—there always seemed to be someone there, even at night."

I sighed. He was right. The lake was popular at all hours, thanks to its romantic reputation. It would have been impossible to ensure he wasn't spotted.

"There was nowhere safe," he continued. "And I'd wrapped him in cheesecloth to camouflage him in case someone did go into the freezer. Later I realized he looked like a mummy. Your sarcophagus seemed like a sign."

"But you could only keep him in your freezer when you were a solopreneur."

And Alex had said he was expanding, hiring staff. How long had that mummy kept him from hiring new staff?

"I tried to warn you off," he said. "I slashed your tires. I waxed your lobby. I thought of broken leg would keep you occupied. But you kept asking questions."

I bit back a hysterical laugh. I'd gotten someone to wax the floors for free. I should have guessed the fastidious caterer was responsible. Knives and cleaning supplies. That was Alex all over.

Stall, stall, stall. But it was futile. No one was coming. "And seeing me here at the Harvest Festival," I said in a monotone, "was that a sign too? Did you just *happen* to follow me into the festival vineyard?"

"No," he said. "I was going to your apartment, but I saw you leaving. I followed you here."

Where I'd made it easy for him by walking alone into a secluded vineyard. I was the epitome of every brainless horror movie heroine. All I needed to do next was twist my ankle to complete the cliché. At least I wasn't wearing heels.

I drew my hands from my pockets. If I was going to run, to fight, I'd need them free.

"And Frank Frost..." I said. "He didn't know you'd killed Ira, but he did know about the pay-off, didn't he? Were you the one who suggested he speed things along by paying off the inspectors at Frostova?"

He nodded shortly. "That was before I learned about Ira and my wife."

"Did Frank want to go to the cops about the pay-off?"

Alex's shoulders hunched. "If he had, they would have connected me to it as well, and then they might have learned about Wynnona and Ira. We argued."

"And you shoved him through the window."

"That was an accident," he said swiftly. "I didn't think..." He rubbed his jaw. "I didn't think."

The skin on my arms and chest was clammy. I shivered despite my hoodie. "You left the Ladies Aid kitchen window unlocked the night before the soft opening. You came back when everyone was gone and brought Ira's frozen body through the window that night. That's when you put it in the sarcophagus."

Bringing it in while everyone was going in and out of the hall before the opening would have been madness. But the night before, the unlocked window...

"Ironically," I continued, "the door to the hall wasn't locked. You would have had an easier time of it that way, and not left any traces behind. It couldn't have been easy getting a man's frozen body through. Did you worry you'd left traces of Ira behind on the frame? Is that why you set the Ladies Aid kitchen on fire?"

The melted can I'd found... I hadn't recognized it earlier, but I was pretty sure now it had been canned heat, like in that balloon at the science fair. It was something else a caterer would use. He'd used them to heat the chafing dishes at the soft opening.

I glanced around the vineyard. We were still alone. No one had come. My body grew heavy.

"And now what?" I asked. "You can't *accidentally* kill me."

"I can't lose Wynnona." He stepped closer. "She doesn't know I know. She wants to make it work now. We can have everything back the way it was."

"You can't go back, Alex," I said. "None of us can."

"We can be a couple, like we were. I can't lose her now."

"I think you already have." Hands shaking, I pulled out my phone and glanced at the number I'd randomly dialed. I blinked, surprised. *Mason?* "I wasn't recording the conversation, but someone was listening." I extended the phone toward the caterer.

Even in the weak moonlight, I could see the blood drain from Alex's face. He took a step backward.

There was a masculine shout. A muscular silhouette raced between the grapevines toward us.

Alex tensed.

"Don't run," I said quietly. "There's nowhere to run, and you'll only make it worse."

The man didn't slow. Mason plowed into Alex, tackling him to the ground so hard I had to jump out of their way.

Mason rolled Alex onto his stomach and pinned one arm behind him. He jammed one knee into the caterer's ribs. "You okay?" Mason asked, crouching on the earth. I thought I could smell it, dry and comforting.

Mason held one of Alex's arms tucked awkwardly against his broad chest. His face was craggy in the moonlight. The noise from the festival flowed quietly around us.

"Maddie?" Mason's eyes gleamed Adriatic blue.

Willing my heart to return to its regularly scheduled beat, I nodded. But I didn't feel all right. It would be a long time before I felt all right. It was easy to say Jason and I'd let each other go, but harder to believe it.

Mason gazed at me, his blue eyes steady. My throat tightened.

But I was alive. I was lucky. Mason had come for me. I had friends. Mason and Adele and Harper and Leo and even Herb. I nodded again. "I'm fine."

chapter thirty-one

SPIRIT PHOTOGRAPHS

United States, circa 19th century

The mass deaths during the American Civil War led to an increased interest in spiritualism in general and spirit photography in particular. These images by photographers William Mumler and William Hope depict their clients with the supposed spirits of their departed relatives.

Halloween at a paranormal museum is an exercise in gilding the lily. So I'd decided to keep the focus on the exhibits. Our grand opening decorations had been limited to jack-o-lanterns. Lots of jack-o'-lanterns.

We'd cleaned out a local pumpkin patch. I'd hired three temps, including Jordan, to keep up with the carving. And if I never carved another pumpkin, it would be too soon. Standing beside an antique spirit cabinet, I massaged my hand.

Jack-o'-lanterns lined the tops of the walls. They grimaced down at the costumed guests weaving through the passages. Gangs of jacks hung out in gloomy corners and leered around corners. There were hundreds of them.

I was in my paranormal museum gear. Our grand opening was a photo opp. I wanted as many pics of the museum ghost logo as I could get. A local makeup artist had done up my face to look like a ghoul. The effect was startling and itchy.

Black and white photos—spirit photography from the 1860s and 1870s—hung on the elegant charcoal walls. Pedestals displaying tools of the 19th-century medium's trade dotted the space.

A photographer from a San Francisco paper snapped a photo of Herb holding up a spiritual telegraph dial. The flash turned Herb's coke-bottle glasses to pale moons.

A woman in a corner with a blue camera on a tripod snapped a portrait of a seated guest. At a small, nearby table, her partner read another guest's aura photograph, explaining what the colors meant.

Adele, dressed like a witch, nudged me. LED lights blinked purple in the black feathers crowning her pointed hat. "It's a success."

"Did you have any doubt?" Harper, dressed like a town councilor in a burnt-sienna pantsuit, sipped her champagne from a plastic glass. Her t-shirt read: *THIS IS MY COSTUME.*

I swallowed. Now that Alex's catering business was no more, our down payment was in the wind. I hadn't been able to find a caterer for the night we could afford. So we'd stuck with drinks. It was enough.

I'd explain about the vanished down payment to the board later.

"Thanks for keeping the paranormal museum display in the tearoom's bookcase," I said to Adele. "It's helped get the word out."

The secret door between our spaces would eventually be moved here. I was planning to put it to use as a puzzle experience for guests, a door to a hidden supernatural world.

"I notice the Egypt display is gone," Harper said.

My hand automatically rose to scratch my face. I forced it to my side. "The sarcophagus was the best part of the display."

"You got it back though," Harper said. "Didn't you?"

"Yes, but displaying it didn't seem right." It would have attracted a lot of attention, but there were limits to how far I'd go for a marketing promotion.

"Of course not," Adele said. "It wouldn't be right to profit off a man's murder, even if he had been corrupt. What's going on with the investigation at Town Hall?"

Harper grimaced and clawed a hand through her thick, brown hair. "It's ongoing. But Janice from permitting and Mark from the inspections office are on leave for the duration. Unpaid. And this isn't public knowledge, but Janice has confessed."

Adele sighed. "At least she had *some* decency."

"More like the stress finally got to her," Harper said. "When Ira disappeared, she thought Mark had had something to do with it, and *he* thought *she* had. Then when Ira's body turned up in Maddie's coffin—"

"Sarcophagus," Adele and I said automatically.

"Sarcophagus," Harper continued, "they both panicked. They knew the police would be looking at their departments and Ira's doings, and the truth might come out."

"Which is exactly what did happen," Adele said tartly.

"Yeah," Harper said. "Well, apparently Janice doesn't handle pressure well."

"In fairness," I said, "a murdered boyfriend-slash-conspirator is a lot of pressure."

"Speaking of boyfriends," Harper said in a low tone. She nudged my rising arm.

I clenched my hand—I would *not* ruin this makeup—and turned to follow her gaze. Jason and Laurel, dressed as Keystone cops, strolled into the room.

He nodded to me and smiled. Because I could be an adult, I smiled in response. The makeup cracked around my mouth, and my smile turned to an itchy grimace.

Laurel's eyes narrowed, her mouth compressing. She adjusted her tall, black helmet threateningly.

"What are *they* doing here?" Adele whispered.

"The police department wanted a representative at the opening." I preferred to think it was because the opening was an important town event, and not because they anticipated another murderous disaster.

"And they sent Jason and Laurel?" Adele's brows rocketed toward her hat brim.

"They're high-ranking officers," I said.

Adele stepped in front of me, facing me squarely. "And you're sure you're okay with it?"

A sharp ache blossomed in my heart. I breathed into it, and the pain faded. "Yeah. It's a small town. We can't exactly avoid each other. And I'm over it."

This was a dirty lie. Jason still occupied more of my headspace than I should have allowed. But I was going to fake it 'til I made it.

My phone rang in the rear pocket of my jeans. I pulled it out and checked the number. My mother. "Sorry, it's my mom." I put the phone to my ear. "Hi—"

"Madelyn, this is your mother."

I smiled, irritating the skin beneath the thick makeup. "Hi, Mom." She and Cora had successfully fended off the recall election and were stronger than ever. Which was a little terrifying. But I was surprised she wasn't here yet. "What's up?"

"I just wanted to tell you I'll be there in thirty minutes. I was on a call with your sister. It turns out they're *not* having the wedding at the villa. We'll all be staying in a Sicilian castle on the beach. Isn't that wonderful?"

Lightness fluttered beneath my ribs. I'd never stayed at a castle on the beach. "Yeah. That sounds fun."

"I'll see you soon." She hung up.

"Problem?" Harper asked.

"No," I said. "My mom was just delayed with wedding talk."

Chelsea, in an elegant little black dress, strolled into the room with Jordan and a news team. My museum registrar motioned toward a spirit photograph.

The female newscaster said something to Jordan, dressed like a vampire. Jordan straightened and trotted to the photograph. The cameraman followed the boy, who proceeded to expound on... something I presumed I'd catch online later.

"Thanks," Mason rumbled in my ear, and I started.

He wasn't in costume. Mason wore his usual black jeans and tee, though he had on a leather jacket. The night was cold.

I laughed. "You sure you want to thank me? Either Jordan's pumpkin carving skills have leveled up, or he'll never touch another jack-o'-lantern again."

"A little manual labor is good for him," Mason said, "though I think you paid him too much."

"It was what we agreed on," I said, surprised.

"He would have done it for free." He looked meaningfully at Chelsea, who smiled at Jordan. The boy leaned toward her and beamed.

"Is it going to be a problem?" I asked, worried. I knew Chelsea could handle herself. But I didn't want Jordan to get hurt. He'd had enough hurt for a lifetime.

His mother had dropped her bid for custody—at least temporarily—and moved to southern California. Mason had told me she was living with a new boyfriend who didn't like kids.

"Oh, there's Dieter." Adele waved at a lanky figure in a scarecrow costume.

"I want to talk to him about renovating my office," Harper said. The two women ambled across the room.

Mason smiled faintly. "To answer your question, it's no problem. Jordan will figure it out eventually and move on. But if he's bothering her—?"

"No," I said quickly. Chelsea and I had had a talk about Jordan before I'd brought him in as a helper this morning. "She told me he reminded her of her little brother."

Mason barked a laugh. "He'll love to hear that."

"You won't tell him, will you?"

He rubbed his jaw, his hand making scritching noises across the bristles. "We'll see. I'm hoping he'll figure it out on his own and find a new crush who's more appropriate."

"What's the point of an *appropriate* crush?" I asked. "Aren't crushes ridiculous by definition?"

"He's young. One day he'll move past crushes." He pressed one fist to his muscular chest. "And it hurts to think of it, of how much I missed of his life, and how short childhood is."

"Yeah. But it will be all right. He'll be all right." And so would I. Some changes couldn't be stopped, shouldn't be fought. You just had to roll with them and hope.

I met Mason's gaze, and he smiled.

# # # # #

Note from Kirsten:

Last year, I took a class in museum curation, thinking I could use it for these Paranormal Museum mysteries. From that class, I got the idea of the expansion initiated in *Dead End Donation*. I felt like I had to keep writing to get it all out before I forgot what my class notes meant. I wanted to give Herb more play in this book—he's going through some big changes too. But in the end, I couldn't fit it all, and my editors thought I still might have given him a little too much page time. (But I like Herb).

And then... I went to Sicily. I'd planned on using that trip for a honeymoon story (*Revenge of the Ziti*) for Susan and Arsen in my Wits' End series. But there was so much of Sicily I couldn't include in that short story, that I took the other half of the island and used it for the next short mystery in the Paranormal Museum series—*The Cannoli Caper*. There's a castle and a kidnapping and a cat, and yes... cannoli (because it's dangerously delicious in Sicily). And murder.

Apparently mysteries without murders are becoming popular, but I can't seem to be able to bring myself to write one.

So watch for *The Cannoli Caper*, coming in 2024!

Museum Swag Shop!

Be a Paranormal Patron!
Would you like one of Maddie's hoodies? Check out the museum swag shop HERE.
By purchasing our hoodies, t-shirts, and mugs, you're backing the *Perfectly Proper Paranormal Museum* series. Your love for these books fuels future mysterious adventures!

More Kirsten Weiss

THE PERFECTLY PROPER PARANORMAL Museum Mysteries

When highflying Maddie Kosloski is railroaded into managing her small-town's paranormal museum, she tells herself it's only temporary... until a corpse in the museum embroils her in murders past and present.

If you love quirky characters and cats with attitude, you'll love this laugh-out-loud cozy mystery series with a light paranormal twist. It's perfect for fans of Jana DeLeon, Laura Childs, and Juliet Blackwell. Start with book 1, *The Perfectly Proper Paranormal Museum*, and experience these charming wine-country whodunits today.

The Tea & Tarot Cozy Mysteries

Welcome to Beanblossom's Tea and Tarot, where each and every cozy mystery brews up hilarious trouble.

Abigail Beanblossom's dream of owning a tearoom is about to come true. She's got the lease, the start-up funds, and the recipes. But Abigail's out of a tearoom and into hot water when her realtor turns out to be a conman... and then turns up dead.

Take a whimsical journey with Abigail and her partner Hyperion through the seaside town of San Borromeo (patron saint of heartburn sufferers). And be sure to check out the easy tearoom recipes in the back of each book! Start the adventure with book 1, *Steeped in Murder*.

The Wits' End Cozy Mysteries

Cozy mysteries that are out of this world...

Running the best little UFO-themed B&B in the Sierras takes organization, breakfasting chops, and a talent for turning up trouble.

The truth is out there... Way out there in these hilarious whodunits. Start the series and beam up book 1, *At Wits' End*, today!

Pie Town Cozy Mysteries

When Val followed her fiancé to coastal San Nicholas, she had ambitions of starting a new life and a pie shop. One broken engagement later, at least her dream of opening a pie shop has come true.... Until one of her regulars keels over at the counter.

Welcome to Pie Town, where Val and pie-crust specialist Charlene are baking up hilarious trouble. Start this laugh-out-loud cozy mystery series with book 1, *The Quiche and the Dead.*

A Big Murder Mystery Series

Small Town. Big Murder.

The number one secret to my success as a bodyguard? Staying under the radar. But when a wildly public disaster blew up my career and reputation, it turned my perfect, solitary life upside down.

I thought my tiny hometown of Nowhere would be the ideal out-of-the-way refuge to wait out the media storm.

It wasn't.

My little brother had moved into a treehouse. The obscure mountain town had decided to attract tourists with the world's largest collection of big things... Yes, Nowhere now has the world's largest pizza cutter. And lawn flamingo. And ball of yarn...

And then I stumbled over a dead body.

All the evidence points to my brother being the bad guy. I may have been out of his life for a while—okay, five years—but I know he's no killer. Can I clear my brother before he becomes Nowhere's next Big Fatality?

A fast-paced and funny cozy mystery series, start with Big Shot.

The Doyle Witch Mysteries

In a mountain town where magic lies hidden in its foundations and forests, three witchy sisters must master their powers and shatter a curse before it destroys them and the home they love.

This thrilling witch mystery series is perfect for fans of Annabel Chase, Adele Abbot, and Amanda Lee. If you love stories rich with packed with magic, mystery, and murder, you'll love the Witches of Doyle. Follow the magic with the Doyle Witch trilogy, starting with book 1, *Bound.*

The Riga Hayworth Paranormal Mysteries

Her gargoyle's got an attitude.

Her magic's on the blink.

Alchemy might be the cure... if Riga can survive long enough to puzzle out its mysteries.

All Riga wants is to solve her own personal mystery—how to rebuild her magical life. But her new talent for unearthing murder keeps getting in the way...

If you're looking for a magical page-turner with a complicated, 40-something heroine, read the paranormal mystery series that fans of Patricia Briggs and Ilona Andrews call AMAZING! Start your next adventure with book 1, *The Alchemical Detective*.

Sensibility Grey Steampunk Suspense

California Territory, 1848.

Steam-powered technology is still in its infancy.

Gold has been discovered, emptying the village of San Francisco of its male population.

And newly arrived immigrant, Englishwoman Sensibility Grey, is alone.

The territory may hold more dangers than Sensibility can manage. Pursued by government agents and a secret society, Sensibility must decipher her father's clockwork secrets, before time runs out.

If you love over-the-top characters, twisty mysteries, and complicated heroines, you'll love the Sensibility Grey series of steampunk suspense. Start this steampunk adventure with book 1, *Steam and Sensibility*.

Get Kirsten's Mobile App

Keep up with the latest book news, and get free short stories, scone recipes and more by downloading Kirsten's mobile app.
Just click HERE to get started or use the QR code below.
Or make sure you're on Kirsten's email list to get your free copy of the Tea & Tarot mystery, *Fortune Favors the Grave.*
You can do that here: KirstenWeiss.com or use the QR code below:

Connect with Kirsten

You can download my free app here:
https://kirstenweissbooks.beezer.com
Or sign up for my newsletter and get a special digital prize pack for joining, including an exclusive Tea & Tarot novella, *Fortune Favors the Grave.*
https://kirstenweiss.com
Or maybe you'd like to chat with other whimsical mystery fans? Come join Kirsten's reader page on Facebook:
https://www.facebook.com/kirsten.weiss
Or... sign up for my read and review team on Booksprout:
https://booksprout.co/author/8142/kirsten-weiss

About the Author

I WRITE LAUGH-OUT-LOUD, PAGE-TURNING mysteries for people who want to escape with real, complex, and flawed but likable characters. If there's magic in the story, it must work consistently within the world's rules and be based in history or the reality of current magical practices.

I'm best known for my cozy mystery and witch mystery novels, though I've written some steampunk mystery as well. So if you like funny, action-packed mysteries with complicated heroines, just turn the page...

Learn more, grab my **free app**, or sign up for my **newsletter** for exclusive stories and book updates. I also have a read-and-review tea via **Booksprout** and is looking for honest and thoughtful reviews! If you're interested, download the **Booksprout app**, follow me on Booksprout, and opt-in for email notifications.

BB bookbub.com/profile/kirsten-weiss

g goodreads.com/author/show/5346143.Kirsten_Weiss

f facebook.com/kirsten.weiss

⊙ instagram.com/kirstenweissauthor/

Other misterio press books

Please check out these other great *misterio press* series:

Karma's A Bitch: Pet Psychic Mysteries
by Shannon Esposito

Multiple Motives: Kate Huntington Mysteries
by Kassandra Lamb

The Metaphysical Detective: Riga Hayworth Paranormal
Mysteries
by Kirsten Weiss

Dangerous
and Unseemly: Concordia Wells Historical Mysteries
by K.B. Owen

Murder, Honey: Carol Sabala Mysteries
by Vinnie Hansen

Payback: Unintended Consequences Romantic Suspense
by Jessica Dale

Buried in the Dark: Frankie O'Farrell Mysteries
by Shannon Esposito

To Kill A Labrador: Marcia Banks and Buddy Cozy Mysteries
by Kassandra Lamb

Lethal Assumptions: C.o.P. on the Scene Mysteries
by Kassandra Lamb

Never
Sleep: Chronicles of a Lady Detective Historical Mysteries
by K.B. Owen

Bound: Witches of Doyle Cozy Mysteries
by Kirsten Weiss

At Wits' End Doyle Cozy Mysteries
by Kirsten Weiss
Steeped In Murder: Tea and Tarot Mysteries
by Kirsten Weiss
The Perfectly Proper Paranormal Museum Mysteries
by Kirsten Weiss
Big
Shot: The Big Murder Mysteries
by Kirsten Weiss
Steam and Sensibility: Sensibility Grey Steampunk Mysteries
by Kirsten Weiss
Full
Mortality: Nikki Latrelle Mysteries
by Sasscer Hill
ChainLinked: Moccasin Cove Mysteries
by Liz Boeger
Maui Widow Waltz: Islands of Aloha Mysteries
by JoAnn Bassett
Plus even more great mysteries/thrillers in the *misterio press* bookstore

Printed in Great Britain
by Amazon

26386922R00126